Books by A. H. Lee

THE KNIGHT AND THE NECROMANCER

BOOK THREE: THE SEA

A. H. LEE

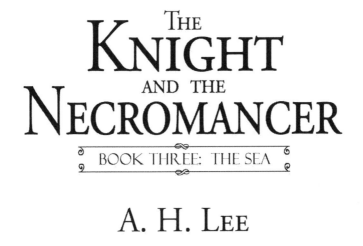

Pavonine Books 2020

For all my Patreon donors,
who kept asking for more.

1

Bath

By the time they'd finished eating, servants had brought Roland's gear. They'd also found a horse they wanted to show him. Sairis allowed himself to be led through the snowy night to the stables. Roland introduced him to the grooms and made sure they understood that the purchased horse belonged to Sairis. The animal did seem quite gentle—a shaggy chestnut who had clearly never missed a meal, just tall enough to be called a horse and not a pony. Apparently, his name was Butterball, but Roland assured Sairis that this could be changed.

He made Sairis saddle the animal once, just to make sure he knew how. It took him a few moments, but he eventually got everything fastened correctly. Roland talked about the nutritional requirements of horses, how to care for them at night, basic hoof maintenance, tack.

Sairis finally pinched the bridge of his nose and muttered, "Roland…"

"I know you know some of this already, but I just wanted to make sure—"

Sairis patted his arm. He looked like he had a lot on his mind, possibly apart from horses.

"Do you want to go back to the room?" asked Roland.

Sairis nodded.

Roland let him lead the way, making sure that he knew it.

When they arrived, they found their new clothes laid out for them. These were basic garments that had been quickly altered to their specifications, but the fabric was warm and of good quality. Sairis had two pairs of dark trousers, two cream-colored shirts, a charcoal waistcoat, a lighter coat, and a heavy black overcoat. He also had a pair of boots made of supple leather with heavy soles for hiking through mountains. Two pairs of thick, woolen socks lay beside them.

Roland made Sairis try everything on to be sure it fit. In spite of the fact that they'd been naked in each other's arms three nights ago, Sairis seemed suddenly gripped by shyness. He changed clothes without taking off more than one thing at a time and without looking at Roland.

After a moment, Roland said, "I'll just be in the bath. Come and join me when you're finished?"

Sairis raised his head, startled, his shirt half-buttoned. "Bath?"

Roland took his arm and guided him through the bedroom, out the door on the far side, and into a small, walled enclosure. It looked like it ought to contain a garden. Instead, a pool lapped at their feet, the water steaming under the dark, snowy sky. These were natural hot springs, but the stone of the pool had been hollowed and shaped by human hands. The water came in under the wall and exited beneath it on the opposite side. Two lamps marked the far edge of the enclosure, sending a ghostly glow through the steam.

Sairis stared open-mouthed for a moment. Roland wondered if such luxury seemed appallingly decadent to him.

Wicked, even. "It's easy to have these things in the mountains," said Roland apologetically. "They get snow and rainfall here. Not like the plain."

Sairis nodded and turned away abruptly. "I'll just…finish with the clothes."

"There's soap, washrags, and a basin of water in the bedroom," Roland called after him. "They don't actually want soap in the springs, so we do that first."

"I understand." Sairis vanished back into the sitting room and Roland came inside to strip and to do his own duty with the soap and basin. He considered strolling into the sitting room naked and asking Sairis whether he should do a few sword forms first. *But the poor man is feeling conflicted enough already. Give him a moment to himself.*

Roland walked out into the chilly night and stood there with the snow falling on his skin. *"How many friends have you lost this year?"*

He allowed himself to think of all of them and more besides: Marcus, other peers, recruits he'd trained, his father, in many ways his childhood. On this journey through the mountains with Sairis and Marsden, he'd lost a little of his identity: ideas about his family and kingdom, their history with the magicians of Mistala.

I thought we were the heroes. But to look like heroes, we needed a villain. And maybe he wasn't all that different from the man in the room behind me, trying to get up his nerve to take off all his clothes and trust a human being who could hurt him.

You are the premier knight of the realm, whispered a voice in his head, *not the king, not a ruler. You are a tool of power, a sword to cut where you're pointed. Problems of policy are not yours to solve. Trying to do so would only cause trouble for Daphne.*

Roland shook his head. He waded down into the pool, the water deliciously warm on his chilled skin. The hard day's ride seemed to melt away. Roland laid his head back against the warm stone and closed his eyes. He let his thoughts and his limbs drift.

The door creaked. Roland opened his eyes to see Sairis peeking cautiously around the edge. He sat up and grinned. "I thought you might have lain down on the bed and fallen asleep."

Sairis laughed nervously. "There is no chance of that."

"Whatever you're worried about doesn't have to happen."

"I would be disappointed if it didn't."

Roland considered. "Would it help if you could see me, too?"

Sairis swallowed. "Maybe?"

Roland stood up, thigh-deep in the steaming water. Sairis's eyes seemed to grow even darker. Roland stepped out of the pool and stood there on the edge, dripping. At last, Sairis pushed open the door and approached, naked except for his glasses. He was clenching his fists at his sides, as though he wanted to hug himself and was determined not to.

Roland was reminded again of some shy forest creature, infinitely cautious, fearing traps, fearing judgment. He was a fine-boned man, with well-built legs and calves from constantly running up and down stairs. At twenty-two, he'd not yet finished filling out, and there was still a trace of the awkward teenager he'd obviously been. Roland could count most of his ribs, and lamplight drew sharp shadows beneath his collarbones. The way he moved reminded Roland of a deer in heavily-hunted woods.

They looked at each other for a long moment, and then Sairis reached up and took off his glasses with a more human expression of impatience. "Godsdamn it, they're going to keep fogging up."

Roland laughed and walked around the pool.

"They're going to keep fogging up," repeated Sairis, "and I really want to see."

"You could touch instead."

Sairis folded his glasses and crouched to set them on the edge of the pool. He stood up and put both hands on Roland's chest. Roland was reminded of Sairis's hands flat against the other side of a reflection, his face intent. His palms slid over the muscles of Roland's stomach and then around his back to settle there. Sairis's head came to rest against the side of Roland's neck. Roland wrapped his arms around him, his beard a soft tickle.

"I'm not much to look at," murmured Sairis.

"Only the most beautiful thing I've ever seen."

Sairis snorted. "That's because you were a ghost and we were in the Shadow Lands."

"I like looking at you, Sair."

"Well, I *certainly* like looking at you."

"Shall I go through some sword forms?"

Sairis gave a laugh that shook with nerves. "Gods. You might kill me. I'm so cold, it feels like all my blood is already in the wrong place."

Roland let go of him and took a step into the pool. "Get in the water. Then you won't be cold."

Sairis swallowed. "You were…um…right about the bath. I haven't actually been in this much water before."

"Water is heavy. Your tower is tall."

Sairis nodded. "Water is heavy. My tower is tall. The Parabola is a mile away. Rainwater is precious. And wanted outlaws who take off all their clothes for a dip in a stream end up dead." He was starting to shiver.

Roland waited.

Sairis slid one foot into the pool and gasped. He took a step down onto the bench beneath the water, an expression of wonder on his face. An instant later, he was up to his chest. "Oh, gods. Sex can't be any better than this. I'm not even sure massacres are any better than this."

Roland was choking with laughter. "I'm a little disturbed by the order in which you placed those things."

Sairis reached for his glasses again, as though reassuring himself that they were still there. Then he let go of them and dipped his head. He came up gasping. "Whose soul do I have to sell to do this on a regular basis?"

Roland reached out, still laughing, and gathered him into his arms. Sairis turned around and kissed him. His mouth opened in a gesture of trust and invitation. Roland turned him so that Sairis was straddling his lap on the stone bench. He ran his hands down Sairis's spine and over his firm ass, stroked his thighs and hips. Sairis's hands were on his shoulders, in his hair. The feel of their skin sliding together in the warm water was intoxicating.

"Pools are not actually great places for fucking," breathed Roland, trying to remind himself as well as Sairis.

"Why ever not?"

"Because water isn't slippery enough." Roland kissed Sairis again, deeply, loving the way he was trying to get as close as possible on the bench. Sairis's erection bumped against his stomach. Roland's cock brushed his ass.

Roland pushed away from the bench and slid further into the middle of the pool. Sairis tensed. His legs locked around Roland's waist. "It's alright," soothed Roland. "I just thought you might like this better."

In the middle of the pool, Roland's chin was only a couple of inches above the water when standing. It would have been over Sairis's head. But in Roland's arms, with his legs around Roland's waist and his own arms around Roland's neck, he was in no danger. Roland stood still for a moment, letting Sairis get used to the sensation of weightlessness. Sairis had screwed his eyes shut, but now he opened them and looked around. He stared at the courtyard as though seeing it for the first time, at the drifting steam, the soft lights, the dark sky.

"It's a little like the Shadow Lands, isn't it?" ventured Roland.

Sairis spoke in a whisper, "It is nothing at all like the Shadow Lands." He tilted his head back to let the snow fall on his face. Roland kissed his throat.

"Oh…" Sairis's breath shuddered in and out. Roland hiked him up a little in the water, kissing his way over his collar bone and shoulders. Sairis's arms locked around Roland's head, unconsciously rubbing his cock against Roland's stomach.

Roland slid a hand under Sairis's ass, between his spread cheeks and applied gentle pressure to the tight ring of muscle. Sairis made a low groan.

"A hot spring is not good for fucking," purred Roland, "but it's great for helping a fellow relax."

Sairis lowered his mouth to Roland's again. Roland kept touching him, kept kissing. It wasn't long before Sairis relaxed enough for Roland to press one finger inside. No thrusting. Not in water. Just enough pressure to show the muscle what it needed to do. Sairis was breathing deeply, his face flushed with the heat of the water and their lovemaking.

Roland drew back to get a better look. Sairis blinked at him, long lashes beaded with moisture, lips as pink as his cheeks against his dark beard. "Alright?" murmured Roland.

Sairis gave a crooked smile that was equal parts embarrassment and desire. "I feel utterly compromised."

Roland nuzzled under his chin. "Oh, I want to compromise you more." He curled his finger, searching for the sweet spot.

Sairis squirmed against him. "I thought it would hurt, but I just feel a little…strange."

"If it hurts, tell me. It shouldn't."

"I should be afraid," whispered Sairis. "If you drop me, I'll drown."

"I would never."

"I know. Roland, I— Oh!"

"There it is..." murmured Roland.

"Oh, gods, gods, gods... Fuck."

"That's what it's supposed to feel like."

Sairis was trembling. He pushed back against Roland's hand.

"No friction," said Roland. "Not in water. You need to sit on Butterball tomorrow."

Sairis gave a growl of frustration. His teeth nipped Roland's lip. Roland hadn't planned to finish him off yet, but now he wanted to. He removed his free hand from Sairis's back and slid it between them to take his cock.

Sairis groaned into his mouth, his legs quivering around Roland's waist.

How close have I got you? A lot of friction on his dick wouldn't do, either. Roland rubbed him in and out of his sheath. He felt rock hard. Roland's thumb circled the head, pressed into the slit. His other hand pressed firmly into the tight heat of his lover's body. Sairis's kisses faltered, replaced by shuddering gasps. He made a low noise, eyes tightly shut, and his body clenched.

An instant later, Sairis's grip loosened. He slipped down, almost under the water. Roland caught him and held him up.

Sairis gave a shaky laugh without opening his eyes. "This really is how you drown a necromancer."

Roland kissed him on the nose. "You are adorable."

"I feel like I'm going to pass out. Is that normal?"

Roland frowned. "It's the hot water. Let's sit on the side for a moment."

2

Old Memories and New Ones

Roland carried him to the edge, where Sairis dragged himself onto the lip of the pool, his legs still dangling. Steam rose in plumes from his warm skin into the cool air. Roland noticed that he reached out again to find his glasses before settling down.

"You took off your glasses last time, too," he ventured as he heaved himself onto the side. "In the Knave, I mean."

Sairis leaned back on his hands. "I did."

"Does that mean you trust me?"

Sairis tilted his face up. "I suppose it does."

"When I brought them to you," said Roland slowly, "I stopped for a rest beside the road. I was holding them, and I had a dream…"

Sairis glanced at Roland, his expression suddenly guarded. Roland wasn't sure this was the right time to have the conversation he wanted to have. *But what if I never get another chance?*

"I dreamed I was a child chained in a basement," said Roland. "I was afraid, and people had hurt me, and everyone I loved had abandoned me. Then a man came to take me away. He told me to write my name in silver dust. Your glasses are made of silver, aren't they?"

Sairis looked away. After a moment, he said, "Did you... read it?"

Roland reached out to brush a finger over one of Sairis's. "Simon?"

Sairis flinched.

"Harris," said Roland thoughtfully. "S. Harris. Sairis."

"You really do have me tied across your saddle."

"I would never tell. I wasn't even going to tell *you*. I don't mean to threaten you. Only...after what you said about Hastafel's sword, it got me thinking. Was that a memory? What you put in your glasses?"

Sairis hesitated, then nodded.

"Is it like what Hastafel did?"

"A little."

Sairis wasn't looking at him. Roland scooted over and put an arm around him. "Is that child version of you forever reliving that nightmare...so that you don't have to?"

Sairis made a face. He didn't say anything.

Roland hugged him tighter. "Please stop doing it."

"What you saw was a memory attached to my name," muttered Sairis. "It's a safeguard. I can't actually remember my own name when I'm not touching my glasses. I feel like it's on the tip of my tongue. I know it when you say it, but I can't quite remember. That's why Marsden couldn't find my name to bind me when I was in Winthrop's camp. And, yes, my focus contains a piece of my ghost or soul or whatever you want to call it."

A long silence. "Is that the only memory you put in them?" Roland felt he was being cruel, but not speaking his mind would be crueler. *Who else is going to say these things to him?*

Sairis raised and lowered a slender leg from the moving water, watching the steam curl. "I've put a few other memories in there over the years. Things I would rather forget. They make the focus more powerful. And it means I can put those memories and feelings aside whenever I like. When I take off my glasses, I still know those things happened. But it's as though someone else told me the story. I have no concrete pictures in my head, no feelings about them." He shifted on the smooth stone. "I'm not quite whole without those memories, but I'm also not quite..." Sairis trailed off.

Roland waited.

Sairis drew a long breath. "In the tavern, I wanted to be in the *now*. I didn't want some of the feelings I had about your family. So I took them off."

His eyes met Roland's eyes uncertainly. Roland ran a finger over his cheek. "Do you still feel like you need to put away part of yourself to be with me?"

Sairis straightened. He reached over, picked up his glasses and slid them onto his nose. He turned to look Roland in the eyes. "Roland Malconwy, I am in love with you."

Roland actually teared up. He was surprised at himself, embarrassed even. He didn't know what to do, so he kissed

Sairis. When Sairis could breathe again, he said, "I am in love with you against my better judgment, which is what I was trying to say earlier. And I would very much like more than your fingers inside me."

Roland laughed. "I think I fell in love with you that first day. I told myself I was crazy, but I only feel more attached every time we're together. I know you may still break my heart. But it's yours to break." He hesitated. "Please don't do what Hastafel did."

Sairis's face grew still, unreadable.

"Please don't tear yourself apart," said Roland. "You can make better memories. *We* can make better memories. But please let yourself be...whole."

Sairis nodded. Roland thought he might argue or say that what he was doing was better than Hastafel's sword, or different or safer. But he just whispered, "Alright."

Then, to Roland's surprise, he slid back into the water. He looked up over the rims of his foggy glasses, gripping the edge of the pool, and grinned. "I want to do what you did in the tavern."

Oh. Roland allowed his legs to be pushed apart. "Well, I can deny you nothing."

He let out a long breath as Sairis lifted his cock. He'd been hard since Sairis crawled into his lap, although his arousal had flagged during their conversation. Now, the slick wetness of Sairis's mouth made his balls clench. "Gods..."

Sairis was a novice at intimacy, but he was no fool, and he'd been paying attention when Roland sucked him in the tavern. He got his hands busy, rubbing and caressing, his mouth sucking and licking. He took note of Roland's gasps of pleasure and sped up with his breathing. Roland had no doubt that with a little practice, Sairis would have him wrapped around his finger.

Who am I kidding? He already does.

As the pleasure mounted, he stroked Sairis's hair, resisted the urge to thrust against his mouth. "Sair," he moaned. "I'm going to...finish. You might want to...to..."

Sairis took him as deep as he could, looking up at him over his glasses, his dark eyes intent. Roland let himself go. As the aftershocks washed through him, Sairis leaned up between his legs and kissed him. Roland wrapped his arms around him. "You are a wizard."

"That is technically correct."

Roland laughed.

After a moment, Sairis murmured, "Time to go inside? I am reminded that I need to put wards on you."

Roland stood up and helped him out of the water. "Will it take long?"

"No."

"Does it hurt?"

"No. Well, I don't think so. I've never actually done it to another person." He caught himself on a spasm of laughter. "We are still talking about wards, right?"

Roland draped an arm over his shoulders and put his mouth against Sairis's ear. "It takes as long as we've got. It doesn't hurt. Yes, I have done it to another person."

Sairis darted through the door. "Well, then I believe I can do some rather fast spell work."

3

Claimed

Climbing out of the hot spring, Sairis wasn't sure he'd ever felt so relaxed in his life. Or so clean. The contrast of hot water and chilly air had a curiously invigorating effect. Sairis returned to the suite feeling buoyant, not at all concerned with his nakedness. They toweled off beside the door and then Roland suggested they sit beside the fire to finish drying.

Sairis let himself watch as Roland moved around the room. The thick muscles of his thighs and backside were fascinating. *No wonder he doesn't have any trouble staying on a horse up and down all those hills.*

The trace of curls in Roland's blond locks had become more pronounced in the water and steam. Sairis wanted to wrap one around a finger. *Do you ask princes for tokens of their hair? Probably not. That's probably princesses.*

Idiot, whispered a voice in his head. *No sane person gives a necromancer locks of his hair.*

And yet I'm about to ask him for something worse.

With regret, Sairis nipped out of the room to get a few supplies. He returned to find the lamps extinguished and Roland sitting on the rug before the fire. His smile of welcome was as warm as the flames. "Do you need more light than this? I think it's pleasant, but if you need more light—"

"It's perfect," said Sairis. *You're perfect.* He sat down beside Roland, enjoying the warmth on his damp and cooling skin.

Roland glanced at the cup of water Sairis had brought with him. "Is that from the springs?"

Sairis nodded.

"*Does* it have magical properties? The locals swear it will make us live for two hundred years and never get a cold. Also, we'll be terribly virile."

Sairis smirked. "So it's working?" He put a pinch of salt in the water. Then he pricked his finger with a sewing needle he'd found in a bedroom drawer and watched a few drops fall into the liquid. After a moment, he said, "They're not completely wrong. The water's got a bit of an aura. I doubt regular people can access the magic, though. I'm not sure even I can. The Shattered Sea is full of magic and nobody can figure out how to get at it."

He raised the cup, swirling it critically. "It might enhance these wards, though." He murmured a spell, easily channeled through his own blood. It produced a gratifying glow inside the cup. Sairis set it carefully on the floor between them. "I would like some of yours, too. It's not essential, but—"

Roland held out his hand over the cup. Sairis glanced up at him, suddenly reminded of the punch bowl. "I suppose I should advise you that, if letting a necromancer touch you is unwise, giving me your blood is—"

"Sair…" Roland's hand turned over and reached for Sairis's free one. "I trust you."

Sairis gave him a sad smile. "I wonder if you realize how much."

Roland's thumb stroked over his wrist. "I remember the River. You could have told me to do anything. I couldn't think for myself."

Sairis could see that Roland found this unsettling in retrospect. *Good. If you're going to pal around with magicians, you should understand what it means to be bound.*

Sairis cradled Roland's hand in both of his, the tip of the needle against an index finger. He looked into Roland's eyes. "You were kind to me when you thought I was just a shy stranger in a tavern. You pulled a sword out of me and saved my life, even after you knew what I was. You kept our appointment when you thought I was dead, just to say goodbye."

Roland's eyes misted.

Sairis squeezed his hand. "I transferred Marsden's spell to you, and you still came to find me. You handed me my glasses when I was spitting insults at you. You almost let me kill you behind the waterfall."

"Sair—"

Sairis talked over him. "I have never in my life been so lucky in a friend. Don't think I don't know it. I would not hurt you for the world, Roland, but you need to understand that giving me your blood is dangerous. You can say no. I can put wards on you with only my blood, but they won't be as powerful."

Roland leaned across the cup and kissed him. "Have all the blood you want."

Sairis sighed. He pricked Roland's finger and two fat red droplets splashed into the cup. "Your name," said Sairis. "It'll work best if you say it."

"Roland Bertram Malconwy," said Roland.

Sairis hesitated. Then, for the first time in more than a decade, he muttered aloud, "Simon Harris." He activated the spell with words that mundane ears could not parse. Instead, ordinary people interpreted rune-speech as music, often bells, or sometimes visually as smoke or steam.

Roland cocked his head, listening to the strange sounds Sairis was making. The water in the cup brightened even more. "I wish I had a bone pen," muttered Sairis. "Oh, well. Sloppy still gets the job done. Lie down on your back."

Roland stretched out on the rug before the fire. Sairis dotted water onto the crown of his head, between his blue-gray eyes, on the shadowed hollow of his throat. He put a dab over Roland's heart, another at the base of his breastbone, then over his stomach. Finally, he put a dab of glowing water on his cock. It was half hard, and Sairis couldn't resist giving it an extra stroke.

Roland let out his breath in a laugh. "Is that part of the spell?"

"No, I just wanted to." Sairis began the more focused task of writing the runes. It didn't really matter where he wrote them. Roland provided plenty of canvas.

After a while, Roland said, "Do you only have two names?"

"Unfortunately, yes. My parents had a dozen children. I'm sure they were hard-pressed to come up with one name for all of us, let alone two." He glanced at Roland quizzically. "I'm surprised *you* don't have four."

Roland laughed. "I believe my great-grandfather did." He shifted under Sairis's hands, the muscles of his stomach creating distracting ridges. "What are you…doing?"

"Tapping into your innate magical energy. Can you feel it?"

"But…I'm not magical."

Sairis laughed. *Oh, but you are.* "We all soak up magic from the Shattered Sea. Mundanes can't use it, but they've still got it. That's how demons feed. It's why human sacrifices work. It's tied to your ghost…soul…life force, whatever you want to call it. Or some people say it *is* your life force. All very academic."

Roland thought about that. "And these runes protect me from demons?"

Sairis nodded. "From magical attack."

"It feels odd."

"Good odd?"

"I think that's obvious."

Sairis snickered. "Magical transference can have a…stimulating effect."

"Magicians live more interesting lives than I thought."

"Without a doubt."

Roland's cock was hard against his stomach. His nipples had gone a deeper shade of pink. Sairis had a brief fantasy of straddling his hips in the firelight. *Focus.* To distract himself, he asked, "Did your father know about you?"

Roland frowned. "You mean that I prefer men?"

Sairis nodded, now writing across his chest.

"I think so. We never talked about it. And I knew I had to be discreet. But I think he knew."

After a moment, Sairis muttered grudgingly. "I suppose he wasn't all bad."

Roland smiled. He reached up to stroke Sairis's back. Sairis realized that he was, himself, not immune to the side effects of magical transference. *Godsdamn it. Focus.*

Roland was clearly still thinking about Sairis's question. "I'd be lying if I said he approved, but I don't believe he thought he could change me, either. He was a little…disappointed, I think. I suppose that's why I worked so hard at my training, and why I was so keen to go to the border as soon as Uncle Jessup thought I was old enough. I didn't want Father to think he had a soft son, even if I did kiss boys."

Sairis mentally retracted his word of charity for Arnoldo Malconwy.

Roland laughed. "And yet for all my training, I never could be hard in quite the same way as Father and Daphne. Everyone says I take after Mother. She died when I was five in a riding accident. I've often thought I would have felt less alone if she'd lived."

Sairis looked at him curiously. "Were you raised by nannies, then?"

Roland smiled. "I was raised by Daphne! Right after Mother died, I started wetting the bed. My nurse thought she could beat it out of me, and Father didn't stop her. He wanted a tough son. Daphne stopped her. She challenged my nurse to a duel."

Sairis gave a bark of laughter.

"That was how the nurse responded, too," said Roland. "Daphne was seven years old. But she got the switch away from my nurse. There was a scuffle, and Daphne beat her black and blue. The nurse took her complaint to Father, and Daphne steeled herself for whatever was coming. Everyone was surprised when he sacked the nurse."

Sairis smiled.

"My father wasn't the sort of man who told you what you needed to do to impress him," continued Roland. "He just waited for you to do it. Daphne did. A lot more often than I managed to. I doubt Father ever expected to love a daughter as much as he loved her. Even before I was born, I think she'd already convinced him that the laws of succession needed to change. She'd already done the hard work for me, and I didn't even know it. Father didn't need me to be a king. So I suppose it wasn't such a blow that I was an invert."

Sairis spoke at last. "Daphne is a skillful leader, but only a madman could find you a disappointment, Roland. You are the perfect knight!"

Roland smiled. "The perfect knight probably would not chase a necromancer across half the kingdom to return his glasses, ignoring his queen's wishes in the process."

"Did Daphne tell you not to come?"

"I didn't give her a chance. She was displeased after what happened to me with Marsden's spell, but she'll come around when I explain."

Sairis swallowed. Anxiety crept in again.

"Daphne protected me from Father," murmured Roland, "and she's still protecting me. There are so many people who believe I should rule, Sairis. They talk about what a perfect knight I am, and the weakness of women. All Daph would have to say is, 'My brother is an invert. He's not fit to rule.'"

Sairis's wet finger traced runes across Roland's shoulders. He could feel the tension there.

"Finding proof would be child's play for her," continued Roland. "She knows me too well. Her life would be so much easier if I were permanently disgraced. But she doesn't do it. She has never even threatened, not even when we argue."

"You are lucky in your sister," admitted Sairis.

"I'm lucky in a lot of ways." Roland shivered and Sairis could sense the shift in his attention, returning fully to the moment. "Gods, Sair, that...tickles."

Sairis had some idea of what Roland was feeling. *I never take magic from other people,* he realized. *Not living ones.* "Almost done."

Under his hands, Roland's chest gave a hitch. Sairis's cock bumped Roland's thigh and he spoke the final rune in a hiss. Both of their bodies lit with lines of green light. The runes he'd traced onto Roland knit themselves together, bled into the chakra points he'd marked, and then spread outward over Roland's body, crawling across his skin like living things.

Roland's eyes opened wide as he stared up at Sairis, covered in the same spiderweb of runes. Sairis braced himself as the magic leapt between them. He felt Roland's ghost tug gently against his own—a fish on the end of a line, something he could bind or shield. The wards blazed for an instant. Then they began to fade.

"Done," whispered Sairis.

Roland stared up at him. He started to say something. Then Sairis bent over and kissed him. "Take me to bed," he whispered.

Roland was off the rug in a heartbeat. Sairis laughed as Roland first pulled him to his feet and then slid an arm under his knees to lift him. Roland carried him, still laughing, into the bedroom. "I didn't mean literally!"

"Would you like me to put you down?"

"Only if you plan to climb on top of me."

Roland dropped him onto the soft mattress and reached for the dish of oil beside the bed. "We take this slow. I mean it. You've got to ride tomorrow."

They took it slow.

Sairis had never really thought about what it might be like to kiss in a comfortable bed, to feel his lover's weight bearing him down into the mattress, to feel the slide of their cocks together with oil. He'd never thought much beyond an awkward kiss in a tavern and a quick fumble in the dark. Now, he found that he liked this long, slow build in lamplight. He liked seeing the planes of Roland's body moving above him. He liked the soft mattress, the clean sheets, the privacy, the feeling that they had all the time in the world.

But we don't. This may never come again.

Don't think about that.

Roland's mouth left hot, wet tracks over Sairis's throat, down his belly and chest, playfully licking at his cock, but never to climax. Roland's oiled fingers were patient and eventually more than fingers. By the time Roland pushed a pillow under Sairis's hips and settled between his legs, Sairis was panting with pleasure and frustration, pushing up against him. "Please, Roland. Please, please…"

The sensation of penetration was overwhelming. Roland stopped on the first long slide and looked Sairis in the face. "You put your name on me, didn't you?"

Sairis spoke unsteadily. "Yes."

"Simon."

Sairis shut his eyes.

Roland kissed the hollow of his throat. "You claimed me."

Sairis spoke without thinking. "It feels…the other way… around." *Tied across your saddle, Roland.*

Roland moved again, and Sairis thought he would climax. A sweet tremor washed through him. His legs quivered around Roland's waist. "I don't want you to regret this," whispered Roland. "No matter what you decide to do later, no matter what happens, I want you to know that you are beautiful and lovable and—"

"For gods' sakes, Roland, just fuck me."

Roland sped up. Sairis threw his head back and cried out. The pleasure built and built until Sairis thought he couldn't stand it anymore. Roland was going to fuck him right across the River, and he couldn't think of a better way to go. He tried to get a hand between them and Roland pinned it over his head. Sairis caught his breath on a sob. The muscles of Roland's torso were hard as steel under his shaking thighs.

"Sair…" panted Roland. His rhythm faltered and he let go of Sairis's wrist.

Sairis caught him around the neck and spoke in his ear. "Want you inside me," he breathed.

His words had an immediate and gratifying effect. Roland groaned and his body shuddered. But before he withdrew, he heaved himself up on one massive arm and slid a hand between them. Two strokes was all it took. Sairis convulsed. His eyes watered with the intensity of the pleasure as it spilled in hot spurts across his stomach and chest.

Some time later, after they'd had another dip in the springs and lay in drowsy contentment, Roland murmured, "You know the way to the stables. And you have supplies and a horse. I'll fall asleep in a moment. If you aren't here when I wake up…I'll understand."

Sairis pressed his face into Roland's neck, one arm wrapped around his chest. But he didn't say anything. *If I had to wear a mage collar to have this forever…would I?* He was still thinking when Roland's breathing grew deep and even, his heartbeat slow and steady under Sairis's head.

4

Gifts from Marsden

Roland woke to the soft chiming of the bell rope. He sat up and gave an answering tug to show that he was awake. The air outside the sheets was chilly, the spot beside him in the bed cold.

Gone.

Roland swallowed. *I will think about it later. Today: Daphne, Winthrop, my men in the pass. If I die in battle, my feelings will not matter. If not, I will have the rest of my life to think about Sairis. Plenty of time for that later.*

The idea produced an unexpected tightness in his chest—a sense of resistance, as though the drawer of "things for later" was becoming rather full. He took a deep breath.

"Roland?"

Roland raised his head. A figure was framed in soft light from the next room.

Oh. Roland scrubbed hard at his face.

Sairis came padding over to the bed in his socks. He was wearing his new dove gray waistcoat, white shirt, and fitted trousers. He had his sleeves rolled up, a cup of tea in one hand. He looked wonderfully domestic.

Roland tried to sound casual. "You're still here."

"Yes, they set out breakfast for us before the bell, and I woke up." He came quickly over to the bed. "I'm sorry, Roland,

I didn't mean for you to wake up alone." He got a better look at Roland's face, put his tea down on the bedside table, and hugged him. Roland pulled him down across his lap, and Sairis laughed.

"You're still here," repeated Roland.

"I'm still here. Do I look like I'm playacting in these clothes? I feel like it."

"You look extremely handsome and respectable. Also good enough to eat."

Sairis wrapped his arms around Roland's neck and slid a knee over his lap. His body felt relaxed and trusting. Roland pulled him up close, enjoying his warmth through the sturdy fabric. "I wish we had all morning. I would utterly ruin these clothes."

Sairis snickered. "Run away with me?"

"I wish I could. Thank you so much for staying." He stroked Sairis's hair, ran a hand over his back. "How do you feel? Up for riding this morning?"

"I feel like a knight pinned me to his bed and ravished me until I couldn't see straight." Sairis pulled back enough to let Roland see his smirk.

Roland kissed him. "I take it that's not a bad thing."

"I wouldn't trade it for any other feeling in the world."

A knock on the door interrupted a heated kiss that might have led to things they didn't have time for. With regret, Roland let Sairis disengage and go to answer the door. He got up and began to dress, noting with amusement that Sairis had once more left him in need of a cool, calming bath and perhaps a few moments of meditation. Roland felt as though his desires had been sleeping for the last year, buried in the icy mountains. Now, suddenly, he was awake again.

Sairis stepped back into the bedroom a moment later. "It's Marsden. He seemed to think we...um...might not get going on time."

Roland laughed.

Sairis looked a little pink around the ears. "He wants a word with you."

* * * *

When Roland stepped into the sitting room, Sairis took his tea to the desk and sat down. He fished a handful of folded paper charms out of his pocket. He'd lost everything apart from his glasses after Marsden kidnapped him. Until this morning, he hadn't had a moment to himself to begin rebuilding his arsenal of half-finished spells.

Sairis's magic had not fully recovered from calling the River through Hastafel's sword, but he had enough for a few small things. The inn had thoughtfully provided paper, pen, and ink, and the water from the spring did have some excellent anchoring properties. Sairis had been at work over breakfast, and now he continued, occasionally pricking his finger for a drop of blood as he folded the charms.

He *could* feel the physical ache of his night with Roland, not just in his backside, but throughout his entire body. Muscles not accustomed to being used with such abandon burned as though he'd been running or swimming. *But it is a wonderful sort of discomfort.* He would not have traded it for all the magic in the Shattered Sea. *I have made the right decision,* thought Sairis.

I am a man and a human being, and someday I will go down the River just like everyone else, but right now, I want to live. *I will not spend my life hiding in a tower, wondering what might have been.*

In spite of their late night, Sairis's mind felt sharp and clear. He had no difficulty focusing on his work. He wasn't sure how much time had passed when Roland came up beside him and put a hand on his shoulder. "We're almost ready to leave, Sair. Marsden needs to talk to you about something. I want you to listen to him. You may not like it at first, but just…hear him out."

Roland was dressed in his new clothes, his hair brushed and gleaming in the lamplight against the dark fabric of his coat. Sairis could not quite read his expression.

A hint of uncertainty stirred as Sairis swept the paper charms off the table and stuffed them into his pocket. "Alright."

His uneasiness grew as he came into the sitting room. When he'd met Marsden at the door, the other magician had been wearing his travel cloak with the hood up against the falling snow. Now Sairis saw that Marsden was dressed in formal attire—a linen and lace cravat above a dark maroon waistcoat with silver buttons and cufflinks to match. His overcoat had a high, elegant cut. He'd put on a court wig with garnets.

Sairis had grown used to the grumpy old man in rumpled travel clothes who treated him like a prodigal child and was pleased to be called Andrew. This person, however, was clearly Lord Marsden, dean of magical studies at Mistala University. He looked like the sort of person who had no truck with demons or werewolves and who bound sorcerers and necromancers every day before breakfast.

Sairis knew that he himself ought to feel respectable in his new clothes, but he didn't. He felt like what he was—a practitioner of death magic who knew more about ghosts than any living person ought to know.

Marsden and Roland had clearly been eating breakfast as they talked. Marsden was still sipping a cup of tea, although he'd gotten to his feet. He set down his tea and looked at Sairis critically. "Roland tells me that he made your escape easy last night, Sairis, and you chose to stay with us."

Sairis nodded hesitantly.

"Are you willing to help in the battle against Hastafel?"

Sairis felt a prickle of irritation. "I went into the sword, didn't I? I called the River to save you!"

Marsden's gaze didn't flicker.

Sairis took a deep breath. "Yes."

Marsden nodded. "I have concerns about the situation we may find in camp. Lord Winthrop is not to be trusted, but if we of Mistala turn on each other now, our discord could be fatal. Winthrop's men are loyal to him. Many of the border lords are of his age and have fought wars alongside him. Daphne's throne is new and her position as the first female monarch is precarious. We must not pick fights at this moment."

Sairis shut his eyes, took a deep breath. "I understand. I will not...seek revenge."

"I'm afraid your mere presence will be extremely divisive." He reached into his pocket and pulled out something that flashed silver.

Sairis's chest gave a squeeze. Marsden held a collar that shown in the lamp light—not iron, but spelled steel. *I can't melt that.* Runes looped and curled over the gleaming metal— a sophisticated shackle for a dangerous monster. *He must have spent all night making it.*

Marsden was still talking, but Sairis couldn't focus. There was a roaring in his ears. His vision darkened around the edges. He took a step back and came up against Roland's immobile bulk. Roland's large hands folded around his shoulders. "Sair, listen to what he's saying."

Sairis was trembling. *They're going to put it on me. I'm still too weak to fight. I'll be helpless. They'll put it on me, and they'll do whatever they like with me. Because I didn't run when I could have.*

Roland was talking. Sairis could feel his voice rumble through his chest, but the words were meaningless. *Everything Marsden says will be reasonable—kind, even—and Roland will agree with him. It will all make sense, and they will put that collar on me, and I will never do magic again...*

"Sairis!" Marsden was right in his face. "You are panicking, kid! Calm down! Look at it! Look!" He thrust the collar into Sairis's hands.

Sairis was shaking so hard that he almost dropped it.

I am going to beg. I'll hate myself later, but I am going to...

Sairis blinked. The collar was not as cold as he'd expected. Spelled steel always felt so cold to his magical senses. This felt...

ordinary. Sairis squinted at the collar's aura. It was definitely enchanted and it definitely had Marsden's mark upon it. The runes were powerful symbols of binding, and yet the aura did not quite match them.

"What…?" He turned the collar over in his hands, closely examining the runes. At last, Sairis looked up into Marsden's dark blue eyes, his mouth falling open. "An illusion?" he whispered.

Marsden gave him a crooked smile. "As I just said about five times."

Sairis's gaze fell to the collar again, amazed.

"I realize it was unkind to show you before telling you," continued Marsden, "but I've never tried this before. I wanted to see whether it would fool you at a glance. If it fooled you, I believe it will fool others."

"It fooled me," said Sairis faintly. "What… What is it made of?"

"Tin."

He really must have worked on it all night.

Sairis had tears in his eyes when he looked up again. "I am very sorry I set you on fire, Andrew."

Marsden's laugh was rough. "I believe you are on our side and that you are in control of your own essential nature, Sairis. You are going to walk into that camp there with all of your considerable destructive abilities intact. Please don't make me regret it."

5

Unity

It didn't take Sairis long to realize what a gift Marsden had given him. As he rode into the war camp atop Butterball's rolling back, men reached for weapons. Swords emerged from scabbards, spears were hefted, crossbows loaded, arrows set to bowstrings. A handful of mages came running with half-formed spells in their fists and on their lips. But the moment they saw the collar, the weapons came down. Fireballs vanished. Binding spells remained unspoken. The attention of the guards shifted fully to Roland and Marsden. A collared necromancer was not a threat. Sairis as a mere man was so unintimidating that nobody even suggested he be tied.

He watched as royal guards greeted Roland ecstatically, bowed deeply to Marsden…and ignored Sairis entirely. Messengers galloped away. As the three of them advanced through the layers of pickets around the camp, the news of their coming began to precede them. More and more important people arrived to pay their respects. They'd just entered the camp proper, when a guard in royal livery pounded up to say, "Your Highness, the queen is delighted to hear of your arrival and anxious to see you." There was an edge to his voice, as though he was delivering something a bit stronger than an invitation.

Sairis sensed more eyes on him as they moved between the thickly staked tents in the dawn light. Men lined the way or stared from behind canvas flaps. He caught whispers.

"The prince got him, then."

"…spent three days hunting him down…"

"Glad Lord Marsden made the collar this time."

"Hope they plan to execute him."

Sairis forced himself to keep his eyes straight ahead. *I could get away. I could burn them all.*

Although…maybe I already did?

He wondered whether any of these soldiers had spent an evening putting out necromantic fire and chasing down undead elk. *I certainly know how to make friends, don't I?*

The royal tent loomed ahead, bright banners snapping against the pink dawn glow. The guards at the entrance had arrows trained on Sairis as he dismounted. There was a brief argument at the flap. "The necromancer stays outside."

"He's collared," snapped Marsden. "Are you blind?"

"He comes inside or I don't," said Roland.

The guard disappeared with a scowl. An instant later, he reappeared and ushered them through the flap, across a dimly lit space, and into a smaller tent within the larger one, where the queen waited.

The space was almost bare apart from a couple of standing lamps. Sairis had the impression that people had been packing to leave. There were still rugs over the canvas floor and marks where furniture had sat. Daphne was dressed in no-nonsense furs and riding leathers. She'd taken the bold step of wearing trousers, which Sairis supposed indicated that she intended to be among the real business of the battle, not waiting in the rear for news.

Her face was set in a stern glower, but her posture broke when she saw her brother. She crossed the tent in three strides. "Roland!" They embraced for a moment in silence. One of Roland's hands cradled her head. Daphne's fingers fisted in the fabric of his shirt.

Sairis could see her visibly pull herself together as she stepped back. "You have made the last few days difficult, Brother."

"I'm sorry," said Roland. "I can explain—"

"Uncle Winthrop has told me such a story," continued Daphne, her eyes darting to Sairis. "I do not know what to believe, and there is very little time for explanations. Anton, Uncle Jessup, and I are riding into the pass within the hour with plans to attack Hastafel's troops at dawn tomorrow. Winthrop will take our border lords down the Valley of False Hope to hit Hastafel in the flank as we draw him forward. There is tension between Anton's troops and our border lords. I will be pleased to see them separated. If we win a battle together, I believe this tension will ease, but in the meantime, we are not all feeling entirely trusting. Your actions, Roland—"

"Uncle Winthrop took Sairis," hissed Roland. "He ordered Marsden to capture him while he was spirit-walking in the mirror, to take him without your knowledge or consent. He misled us to think Sairis had run away. The moment I figured it out, I went after him, Daphne. I'm sorry. I just couldn't wait."

Daphne put a hand to her temples. She took a slow breath, let it out again. "This is, of course, not the story I have been told, and for all I love you, brother, your judgment regarding this person is suspect." Her eyes flicked to Sairis with a look that said, "I'll deal with you later."

"Uncle Winthrop thinks you are weak and unfit to rule," said Roland tightly. "He told me as much when I demanded he return Sairis out of deference to your stated wishes. He then…" Roland's eyes skipped around the tent, at the door, where guards might be listening in spite of their low voices. He leaned over and spoke in Daphne's ear.

Sairis hoped he was telling her that Winthrop knew Roland's secret, that he'd tried to make Sairis his spy. Control over Roland would be the next best thing to control over the throne. Daphne's eyes opened wide and Sairis felt certain that Roland had stated the case accurately.

Her eyes flicked to Marsden, who inclined his head. "You set me to play a role, Your Grace. I felt that role was best served by continuing in the confidence of his lordship in the matter of Magus Sairis. I did not realize the…connection with Roland until the events surrounding Sairis's escape from Winthrop's camp. If I had had more information, I would have behaved differently."

Sairis sensed the subtle rebuke in Marsden's tone. *Well, no one will say you weren't brave, Andrew.* Daphne's scowl could have liquified steel. Sairis remembered her conversation with Marsden in the kitchen of the Tipsy Knave. *He's right. She could have told him more. But he could have told her more, too. We all need to trust our friends more, apparently.*

He took his courage in both hands and spoke. "It is true that I panicked when Marsden came after me, Your Grace. I believed I had been betrayed. I made something of a mess in Lord Winthrop's camp when I fled. But I never wanted to harm Roland. Lord Marsden and I have spoken of these things more calmly over the last few days, and I see that we've had several misunderstandings. You may not believe me, but I *am* on your side, Your Grace."

Daphne's gray eyes locked with his. She opened her mouth, but never got to speak, because at that moment, a flurry of sharp words arose outside the tent flap. Sairis heard a familiar voice, full of cool authority. "I will announce myself, thank you." Lord Winthrop strode into the tent, despite weak protests from the guards.

He made a bow that seemed entirely perfunctory. "Your Grace, I must question your decision to meet with these people under so little protection."

"And I question your decision to enter my chambers unannounced."

There was a startled silence. Sairis had the impression that Daphne had not directly rebuked her eldest uncle in quite this way before. He seemed off-balance for a moment. "Magus Sairis is collared, as you can see," continued Daphne.

"A collar he chose to wear voluntarily," added Marsden.

Sairis's eyes flicked to Marsden's face, but the elder mage did not spare him a glance.

"So, you see," continued Daphne to Winthrop, "there is no need for a high level of security. I did not request your presence.

However, since you have joined us, perhaps you would like to speak for yourself regarding Sairis's removal from the inn where he'd been performing tasks I commanded. Did you, in fact, order Marsden to take him without my knowledge and against my expressed wishes?"

If anyone had expected Winthrop Malconwy to cower under this thinly-veiled accusation of treason, they were disappointed. His sharp eyes surveyed them one by one. His big, battle-scarred hand stroked his beard. "You don't want to go down this road, Your Grace."

"I strongly advise *you* do not go down a road of telling me my wishes, Uncle. My throne is new and about to suffer an extreme test. My need for unquestioned loyalty is dire. Some would advise me to make an example of a high officer. To show I will not be trifled with. Do not suppose that I am too weak or 'womanly' to start this campaign with a traitor's head on a pike."

That penetrated. Winthrop went very still.

Daphne continued in a voice of ice, "I would, however, prefer unity. I will accept an apology. I will not be offended by the truth, no matter how treasonous, if you begin *right now*."

Sairis held his breath. He wondered what it must be like for Winthrop—a proud man who'd fought and killed while Daphne was still in nappies—to receive such a rebuke from his niece. It might backfire…

"Did I remove the necromancer from an inn?" said Winthrop slowly. "You mean the Tipsy Knave?" he said the name as though holding it by two fingers. "A well-known haven for inverts and practitioners of buggery?"

Sairis's stomach did a sickening flop. *Of course. This was always coming.*

Out of the corner of his eye, he saw Roland stiffen.

"I understand why a necromancer might seek refuge in such a place," continued Winthrop in studied tones. "One sort of degeneracy doubtless breeds others. But how did *you* come to seek refuge there, Your Grace? I've had disturbing reports over the years of someone very like my nephew going there quite often, although of course I gave such reports no credence. But I do believe I could produce a remarkable number of witnesses… if I were so inclined."

"Such things are not illegal, Uncle." Daphne spoke without inflection. "I fail to see what gutter-rumors have to do with your refusal to follow my instructions about a magician who was promised safe passage in our capital."

"Not illegal *now*," murmured Winthrop. "Not since my brother made a few scribbles in the law. But our border lords all remember when such degenerates were thought little better than animals to be hunted. And while the law may have changed a few years ago, the minds of men change more slowly, Your Grace."

"Are you threatening me, Uncle?"

He shrugged minutely. "I didn't think so, Niece. Perhaps you misheard."

"You have not—" she began, and this time he dared to interrupt her.

"Unity, as you say, is vital for Mistala at this juncture. If we fight amongst ourselves here in the pass, Hastafel and his minions will eat us alive. If you make the misguided decision to put my head on a pike, I will have a few things to say at my execution. I promise, they will not bring unity. Laws of female succession are as new as those regarding perverts. The lords have accepted the former, but I think you'll find they're still fairly unconvinced about the latter. I promise you do not want a close examination of my brother's motives in changing these things, *Your Grace.*" All the deference was gone. He was speaking to a child.

Sairis saw with a pang that, though Daphne was seething, she wasn't sure how to answer him. *He really does have her in a corner.*

Sairis risked a glance at Roland, who looked stricken. Sairis wanted to go to him, hold him close and tell him, "You are perfect. There is nothing wrong with you. These people are insane." *If Winthrop uses Roland to break Daphne, Roland will never get over it.*

Another disturbance outside the flap, and a new man walked into the tent. Sairis didn't recognize him, but he knew at once that this must be Jessup. He was a few years younger than Winthrop, but he looked older with a careworn face, bald pate, and nearly white beard. He had a long scar across his cheek, and his right hand appeared to be missing a finger. Jessup had been defending Mistala from an invading army for five brutal years on unforgiving terrain, and it showed.

His voice, when he spoke, was rough, but mild. "Roland, it is good to see you. The men miss you."

In spite of his obvious distress, Roland broke into a hesitant smile. "I have missed them, sir. I am sorry to have been away longer than intended."

"I was just looking at Cato," continued Jessup placidly, as though the whole tent didn't feel like a box of kindling waiting for a match. "His gait is a bit off."

Roland grimaced. "We rode hard to get here. He carried two riders over broken, mountainous ground for the better part of three days."

Jessup nodded. "I don't believe he's injured, but he's in no shape to carry you in full armor. You'll need another horse for the battle. I'll see to it." He glanced from Winthrop to Daphne, his eyes skating over Sairis and Marsden. "My Queen…Gentlemen…I speak from experience when I say that the tension of battle can bring out our worst natures. Thousands of men are about to risk their lives, and they are counting on us to lead them with integrity and clear heads. May I give my humble counsel that we put aside discord until after this battle? Our disputes may seem less important after that."

Winthrop and Daphne both blinked. Everyone in the room shifted a little. "Your counsel is wise, Uncle Jessup," said Daphne. "I will withhold final judgment about the things I have learned this morning until we have dealt with our enemy. Perhaps a few nights' sleep will give all of us better perspective." She glared meaningfully at Winthrop, who bowed.

"I may have spoken rashly," he said without quite looking at anyone. "I agree that arguing now could cost needless lives."

"I've been thinking," continued Jessup. "If Roland is here, I suggest he lead my troops from the fort. They love him, and he knows the terrain."

Daphne frowned. "Do you plan to be doing something else, Uncle?"

Jessup nodded. "If Your Grace agrees, I think I might go with Winthrop to help guide his men over the difficult ground."

"You've already given us a guide," said Winthrop.

Jessup nodded. "Yes, but it is a complex route, and I think a small party from the pass, led by myself, would be more certain of bringing the border lords in at the right moment."

His bright eyes flicked around the tent. *He's offering to supervise Winthrop,* thought Sairis. *Good idea.* He didn't know Jessup at all, but he already trusted him more than his elder brother.

Winthrop didn't like it. That was obvious. But he couldn't disagree without sounding like he intended something nefarious. "Is the necromancer still to be used in the battle?" he asked instead.

"Magus Sairis has offered his services in the battle, yes," said Marsden. "I will ensure that he has access to his magic at the appropriate time."

"In that case, I ask that he accompany my party. He'll be more useful after the battle has started anyway. More dead on the field. Our point of attack should be ideal for that."

No. Sairis looked at Roland, but Daphne was already speaking. "I will concede that is true."

"Daphne," began Roland, but her eyes snapped to his face with such a look that he shut his mouth.

Winthrop just wants to split us up! A little voice in Sairis's head whispered, *Maybe Daphne wouldn't mind splitting us up, either.*

"We are agreed, then," said Jessup. "Roland will lead my troops, who will accompany Lamont and the queen. I will lead the scouts who guide Winthrop's men up the valley and Magus Sairis and Lord Marsden will accompany us. Daphne, I believe Lamont's forces are ready to ride. Roland, the armory can outfit you, but you'll want to hurry. I've already thought of the right horse. Meet me at the stables?"

"Yes, sir," said Roland in a distracted voice.

"I have preparations to make as well," said Winthrop. "Good day, Your Grace."

When the uncles were gone, Roland said desperately, "Daph…"

She had her arms crossed, clearly lost in thought. "Roland, you need to get moving."

Roland looked miserable. He turned to Sairis.

Sairis forced himself not to make a scene. "I'll be alright."

Daphne screwed up her face. "For gods' sakes, Roland, it is for two days!"

Roland looked like he wanted to cry. "I'm sorry," he whispered to Daphne, "about…about what Winthrop said…"

"Don't," said Daphne in a tight voice. "Don't apologize, Roland. Just go get ready and…and be safe. Please."

Roland looked at Sairis. He glanced towards the tent flap, towards the guards. *I should have hugged you goodbye earlier,* thought Sairis sadly. *I should have known I'd need to.*

Roland dropped a hand on Sairis's shoulder as he passed. It slid down for just a moment to cover his heart. Then Roland was gone.

As Daphne started for the tent flap, Sairis called out, "Your Grace...a word."

He knew what he had to do. He knew, but his hands were shaking.

Daphne looked at him suspiciously, but she stepped closer. Sairis waited until she was right beside him and then whispered. "You have been nothing but kind to me, Your Grace, and I do not want to mislead you. This collar is an illusion."

He shut his eyes as he said it. *She is going to make Marsden put a real one on me. They're going to send me off with Winthrop, collared and helpless.*

A long pause. "Good."

Sairis opened his eyes and looked at her.

Daphne quirked a smile.

Sairis smiled back hesitantly.

She leaned close to his ear and whispered, "You said you are on my side. I believe you. Be careful, Sairis."

He blinked hard and swallowed. "Thank you, Your Grace."

6

Quintin

Two guards stepped in front of Sairis as he emerged from the tent with Marsden. To his surprise, they were not from the border lords, but from the pass. "Commander Jessup has invited you to lodge and travel with his men," said the leader. "He suggests you accept his offer briskly, as another may follow."

He's keeping us out of Winthrop's camp, thought Sairis with relief. *Bless you, Roland's uncle whom I hardly know.*

"We accept," said Marsden at once. "Please show the way." As they led their horses through the tents, Marsden leaned close to Sairis's ear and murmured, "Good job."

Sairis glanced sidelong at him.

"I would have told her," continued Marsden, "when I could be certain of privacy. But if you want her to trust you, well... Good job."

Sairis nodded. He still felt a little queasy, both from the risk he'd just taken and from the sense that he might never see Roland again. "How likely are we to win this battle, Andrew?"

A moment's hesitation. "I don't know, Sairis." Marsden gave him a fleeting smile. "More likely with you than without you."

Then the commander's steward met them with questions about their gear and supplies, and the time for private conversations was over. Several of Marsden's acolytes arrived to speak with him. They cast distrustful glances at Sairis, but obviously had faith in the collar. To Sairis's chagrin, Marsden introduced him to several of these people, including one young woman with a collar that Sairis supposed was quite real. He wanted to ask exactly what sort of "aberrant power" she was and how long she'd managed to tolerate that terrible sense of incompleteness that came when a magician was shut off from magic. But now did not seem the appropriate time, since the students were looking at him as one might a poisonous snake behind glass.

Sairis learned that his performance in Winthrop's camp had injured a dozen people, but killed no one. A fellow whom he vaguely remembered from his imprisonment in the wagon arrived to stare at him sullenly. The man wore a red silk scarf around his head on account of having had all his hair burned away. His eyebrows and beard were gone, too. Magic had mostly healed the burns, but hair could not re-grow so quickly.

Marsden paused to murmur in Sairis's ear, "You have offended that man. He's a magician specializing in potions, part of Winthrop's faction, goes by Quintin. I recommend you avoid him."

Sairis was more than happy to follow this advice, but the moment Marsden stepped away to speak with his students, Quintin made his way over to Sairis. "Lord Marsden keeps quite the collection of freaks," he said without preamble. "I hope that collar's good and tight this time."

Sairis didn't know what to say. *You abducted me and chained me to a cot. If you're waiting for an apology, don't hold your breath.* His fingers were itching for a spell, perhaps muteness. *Steady,* he told himself.

"I understand you put it on yourself this time," continued Quintin. "What did he promise you, I wonder?"

Sairis found his voice. "Mistala is my home, too. I don't like the idea of bending the knee to a dark sorcerer any more than I'm sure you do. You may not believe me, but I came to Chireese to offer my help, and I will give it if I am not continually threatened." *Make friends,* Sairis told himself. *Do not seek revenge.*

"Bend the knee," repeated Quintin. The corner of his mouth twitched in a smile that Sairis didn't like at all. "Rumor has it you do that a lot. Though maybe not for Hastafel."

Sairis felt suddenly out of his depth. *Is this about Roland again?*

But Quintin didn't have the air of a man about to threaten the reputation of a prince of the realm. He had the air of a schoolyard bully in a position of power. He leaned a little closer and murmured, "Death mage… Do you like that? How everyone's afraid of you? Karkaroth hasn't done a thing in twenty years, and the whole country still shakes in its boots every time he sneezes. How does it feel to be helpless now?"

I'm not helpless, thought Sairis, but he felt afraid.

"A collared necromancer on his knees," crooned Quintin. "Now there's a picture. That's spitting in death's eye."

"You're terrible at flirting," Sairis heard himself say. "Also, I prefer men with hair." *Why deny my romantic tastes? These people can't think any worse of me than they already do.*

Quintin's eyes went round with surprise and he jerked back. Sairis forced himself to turn on his heel—no sign of fear—and tug on Butterball's bridle. "I suppose you're leading up to a dinner invitation," he said over his shoulder, "but I've already got one from Lord Jessup, so I must decline. With very little regret, I'm afraid. Truly, you're not my type. Good day."

Quintin's voice snarled after him, "You insolent abomination. You'll regret those words. My Lord Winthrop has plans for you."

"He's not my type, either," snapped Sairis and walked faster.

* * * *

Roland hadn't expected to see his men this early in the campaign. He hadn't realized so many would come from the fort to march with Daphne. Their familiar faces made his heart lift in spite of everything. His lieutenants greeted him with genuine warmth and a hint of relief that sent a pang of guilt through him. *You came back,* their eyes seemed to say. *This can't be a suicide mission. You are with us, so all will be well.*

Roland hoped it was true. The horse they'd chosen for him nickered from outside the tent. The animal was sound and well-trained, but Roland wished he were going into this battle with Cato. He wished he were going with Sairis.

Do Lamont and the border lords understand what we're facing? Truly?

The armies of Mistala had been formidable when this war started. They had been a force to be reckoned with, and now... *We are a few hundred men.*

Hastafel's troops were seasoned from multiple wars of conquest, driven to unnatural feats of savagery by the power of his magic. And one never knew when a monster made of mud or stone might join them. Soldiers who would bravely charge a wall of spears turned and ran at the appearance of those strange creatures with their human voices.

Hastafel had tempted Jessup on more than one occasion to a full assault, but Jessup had always held back. Roland had watched his uncle make the decision to play coy, defend the tight valley, never fully engage. *Because he did not think we could win,* Roland knew.

Now they were going to offer Hastafel what he'd been wanting since the beginning—a winner-take-all battle. *If we offer, he'll accept. He'll throw everything at us.* The idea made Roland's chest tighten.

We'll have the element of surprise with troops coming down the Valley of False Hope. We'll have more men than Hastafel expects with Lamont and all our border lords. Will it be enough?

Roland truly didn't know. But he remembered how the River of Death had risen and swept away six terrifying creatures as easily as a man might swat a gnat. *Sairis did that.* He remembered the burning strategy room, too, the way the dead had staggered to their feet and attacked.

As Roland mounted his unfamiliar destrier and joined his officers and men, following the snapping flags of Mistala and Lamont, he looked back once towards the border lords breaking camp. *I'll miss you, Sair. But I know you'll be there when it matters. I truly think you might make the difference.*

Fort False

The Valley of False Hope had foiled previous campaigns for a reason. Sairis soon forgot about Quintin and Winthrop and even the leaden feeling of separation from Roland as he labored with the rest of the caravan up the rugged, switchback trail into the mountains. He was traveling with Jessup's scouts as requested. Marsden had elected to ride with the commander and some of his acolytes near the front of the group, but Butterball could not keep up. Sairis soon found himself among the supply wagons. He noticed Cato trotting behind one of them, riderless and wearing nothing but a bridle and lead. "Guess we're back here with the invalids," he said to Butterball, and he could have sworn Cato rolled his eyes.

The wagons were as lightly burdened as possible, pulled by powerful mules. Nevertheless, as the trail grew steeper and shrank to a goat path, Sairis could see how they struggled. Their drivers were soon running alongside, clearing stones and sometimes guiding the animals a step at a time. Even Sairis dismounted at last to lead Butterball over the steep, uncertain footing. Behind and below, Sairis could see the train of men and horses, going single file, the heaviest carts in the very rear. Soon, no one was riding. Somewhere below, a horse slipped and fell. Sairis saw the plume of dust, heard the distant screaming neigh. A moment later, the creature's death prickled over his skin. He shivered.

There were no trumpets, no calls, no signals. The whole train moved in near-silence through the rocky, snow-dusted hinterland. Jessup seemed to think it unlikely that Hastafel had scouts out here, but not impossible. Surprise was paramount to their success and so the company maintained very little communication between the front and rear.

The air grew colder and thinner. Men and horses steamed in the icy wind.

Sometimes they stopped as the scouts cleared rocks or fallen trees. Sometimes the scouts gave up and looked for a way around. During these respites, men would sip from canteens or nibble nuts and dried fruit from their packs. Sairis had received his own rations, but what he really wanted was magic. He felt the death of another animal somewhere in the rear, probably injured and put down out of mercy. The splash of energy was like a tease. *More,* whispered a voice in the back of his mind.

Soon, he told himself and felt like a monster.

Frozen waterfalls began to crisscross the trail, making it even more dangerous. After a while, Sairis stopped looking back. He stopped looking ahead. He clutched Butterball's reins in fingers that felt chilly even through gloves, and watched the rear of the horse ahead of him.

The hardest part came at evening, when the light was nearly gone. After a climb that put the horses on their hocks, they had to come down the opposite ridge on loose shale in poor light. Men, horses, and wagons were all covered in the gray dust of the mountain. It stuck to sweat-slick skin, got under fingernails, crusted in the corners of eyes. Sairis thought longingly of warm water enveloping him while he floated in Roland's arms.

When they reached the bottom of the ridge, word came down from the front that they would rest here for the night. Sairis leaned gratefully against his sagging steed. All around him men were pulling bedrolls from saddles. There was little open ground in which to pitch a tent. Instead, it seemed that most of the soldiers would simply sleep on the path.

Sairis wasn't sure how to find Marsden or whether he ought to try. The scout nearest him asked whether he still had water in his canteen and a bedroll behind his saddle. His tone was kindly. Sairis didn't have a bedroll, but he didn't think he would have any trouble just lying down on the path in his clothes and going to sleep.

However, moments later, a messenger edged his way through the men to inform Sairis that he was invited to dinner with the commander. The messenger took Butterball's reins and Sairis followed through the twilight, grimacing as Butterball narrowly avoided stepping on exhausted scouts.

Sairis wondered whether the commander had somehow found space to pitch a tent on the narrow trail. However, as they got deeper into the ravine at the front of the column, the messenger veered off the path into a thick stand of gnarled pines whose roots twisted among the unforgiving rocks. After a winding passage between narrow walls, they arrived at a sturdy wooden gate. "Is this a fort?" asked Sairis in surprise.

"A small one," said the guard. "We call it Fort False because of the valley."

The fort was set into natural caves. It had a small stable, where Sairis took Butterball for a well-deserved nosebag. "You kept up with the big horses," Sairis told him as he removed the tack as Roland had instructed. "Good job."

"Ponies actually do quite well in this terrain," commented the guard from the door.

"I have it on good authority that he is a horse," said Sairis with an attempt at humor.

The guard smiled.

It's so much easier to make friends with the ones I haven't *set on fire,* thought Sairis.

He'd expected to be taken straight to dinner, but instead, they offered him one of the small rooms in the fort with a narrow bed, a surprisingly good mattress, and a wash basin containing clean water. Sairis was aware of the generosity this represented. Even the men in the fort's rough barracks were being given a special dispensation, since space indoors was limited. Actual privacy was so precious and unexpected that it made Sairis's eyes prickle.

With the door closed, he was able to relax and take stock. As he washed in the basin, he thought ruefully that a night of debauchery was perhaps not the best way to begin a punishing march over the most treacherous terrain in the kingdom. *Or, maybe it's actually the best way.* In any event, between the march and his carousing, he felt sore in muscles he hadn't known he possessed. *Will I be able to stand up tomorrow? How embarrass-*

ing will it be if I fall off Butterball and knock myself on the head before the battle?

He could use magic. He had enough to heal sore muscles, although using it would deplete him again. *I'll have plenty once the battle starts,* reasoned Sairis. Still he debated.

Men were hurrying back and forth in the hallway outside his room, having rapid conversations about supplies and broken wagons and lame horses. Sairis lay down on the bed, unsure of whether they'd forgotten him for dinner and not really caring. He dozed off immediately and was awakened a short time later by a scout, sent to bring him to the commander's table.

Sairis sat up and groaned. *This really won't do.* He was going to be too stiff to move soon. Everything hurt, including his hands from gripping the reins. *I won't even be able to write a proper rune.* "A moment," he said aloud.

Sairis stepped from his room an instant later, feeling a bit more alert as well as totally at ease in his body. His magic was so low that he couldn't even get his wards to light up. *But a battle will set my blood alight soon enough,* he told himself. *In the meantime, I will not fall off my horse or down the stairs.* Stairs were quite numerous in the fort, with rooms set into hollowed columns of rock inside the cliff. Sairis's room was halfway up one of these burrowed towers and he got the idea that more important rooms were near the top. It would be easy to defend such a place in the event of attack—lots of narrow corridors where a few men might hold off many thousands. However, the tight spaces made Sairis feel trapped and claustrophobic. He wondered whether there were other exits apart from the main gate.

The officers' mess hall was big enough for about twenty men, and there were at least that many already around the table, eating in a murmur of subdued voices. Everyone looked exhausted. Sairis had been braced for another encounter with Winthrop this evening, whose station must surely entitle him to a bed in the fort. Sairis's fondest hope was that Winthrop might be seated far enough away that Sairis wouldn't have to interact with him.

However, to his surprise, Roland's eldest uncle was not in evidence. Sairis did notice the unpleasant Quintin, talking with a couple of other people who looked like magicians at one end of the table. Lord Jessup sat opposite, along with Marsden on his left. He beckoned Sairis to join them. To Sairis's consternation, the commander motioned to the bench beside him and Marsden made room.

Sairis could feel every eye on him as he sat down, and there was an uncomfortable lull in half a dozen conversations. Lord Jessup pushed a plate of what looked like mutton at Sairis. "Eat, young man. You did well keeping up today, but there will be worse tomorrow. Eat."

Sairis had barely felt his hunger earlier. Now his stomach snarled at the smell of the food. When he failed to do anything more exciting than eat like a starving wolf, the rest of the table slowly returned to their previous conversations.

Marsden gave Sairis a friendly pat on the shoulder as he sat down. However, he was talking to several of the scouts and did not stop to greet Sairis. Jessup was talking to several people on his right whom Sairis gathered were border lords. They were discussing wagons that had broken and the difficulty of moving troops around them on the narrow path. "I do not like this night spent in the open," said one of the lords. "We are exceedingly vulnerable at this moment, Commander."

"I do not like it either," said Jessup, "but I believe that continuing in the dark will be even more dangerous. The men need sleep if they are to give their best tomorrow. We must choose the lesser evil. I was hoping to be closer to the pass than we've managed—to have the fort in the rear of the train, rather than at its front. However, I know the journey has been difficult for the supply wagons. We will not wait for them tomorrow. The wagons will simply have to catch up as they are able."

"I dislike the idea of marching far ahead of our supplies," put in a man with a pinched nose and a wheedling voice. "I recognize that my lords expect a swift victory, but these battles sometimes drag on for days and victuals can make the difference."

"Lamont's troops came down the easier road well-supplied with victuals," observed Jessup.

"I prefer not to depend on Lamontian goodwill," growled another lord, "our queen's new paramour notwithstanding."

Sairis did not like his tone and clearly Commander Jessup did not like it either. "We will not treat our allies as potential enemies, gentlemen. We cannot afford to. And you will not refer to her grace's fiancé as a 'paramour' again in my hearing."

The other lords looked suitably reprimanded, if not convinced.

At that moment, a messenger came smartly into the room and Jessup raised his hand for silence. "Has my brother come at last?" he asked without preamble.

The messenger shook his head. "Sir, I regret to inform you that Lord Winthrop injured his leg when his horse stepped over the edge of the defile. He is riding in a wagon in the rear and cannot come to dinner."

The table went silent with surprise. "What do the physicians say?" asked Jessup after a moment. "Have the magicians looked at him?"

"His lordship's constitution has never agreed with magic, sir, so no magicians. The physicians think he may be able to ride tomorrow with a splint, but they feel it would be best if he were to rest tonight and not move."

Jessup nodded slowly. "When did this happen, and why was I not informed earlier?"

The messenger maintained a neutral expression. "The accident occurred a few hours ago. Communication has been necessarily limited today, sir. The column has become widely separated. Perhaps my lord has not been made aware that it is something around two miles from here to the rearmost wagons?"

Another silence.

"No, I did not realize that," said Jessup wearily. "We are indeed widely separated. Please give my brother my regards and hope for a swift recovery."

A sense of unease washed through Sairis. *Two miles. In country full of rockslides.*

Without thinking, he said, "Sir, how many of these men do you think we will truly be able to bring into the battle in time to make a difference?"

Jessup looked at him in surprise, but he answered without hostility. "I will be happy if we manage to get three quarters of them into the battle at the point her grace would prefer, Sairis. I think half might be a more realistic number. However, I have hope that our trailing faction will continue to reinforce the fight long after we've made our surprise appearance on the field."

This was a more thoughtful answer than Sairis had expected and he felt a little better. Jessup smiled at him, his scarred face pulling at the corner of his mouth in a way that made him look more wistful than pleased. His deep-set eyes studied Sairis long enough for Sairis to become uncomfortable. At last, he said, "I am told my nephew has struck up a friendship with you."

Sairis's stomach dropped in a way that was becoming familiar. But Jessup's gaze didn't seem accusatory or disgusted, only searching. "That is true, my lord," said Sairis carefully.

When he did not elaborate, Jessup continued in a quiet voice, intended for Sairis's ears only, "I also understand that you had some trouble with my older brother."

Sairis licked his lips. He wished Marsden would help him instead of talking to other people. He wished he knew Commander Jessup better. *Why didn't I ask Roland anything about him?*

"I am a necromancer, sir, apprentice to a magician who caused Mistala a great deal of trouble in generations past." The words stuck in his throat, but Sairis was determined not to make a mistake that would damage Roland's future. "I suppose Lord Winthrop could be forgiven for misunderstanding my intentions in Chireese."

Jessup's eyes did not waver. "A generous position. You do not resent being forcibly collared?"

Something in Jessup's face made Sairis afraid to lie to him.

"I wish I could say I was so high-minded, sir. Roland might be able to overlook such a thing. I, on the other hand, melted my mage collar, created a few undead elk to attack people, and set your brother's camp on fire."

Jessup's mouth twitched up, and Sairis knew he'd hit the right note of honesty.

"As," Sairis added, "you have surely been told, sir."

Jessup nodded. "You ran. And then you came back. With a collar that I'm told you chose. Did Roland have anything to do with that?"

I could swear you're asking whether I love him. "I would never have come back if Roland had not procured my…" Sairis had been about to say "goodwill." But Jessup's eyes pinned him to the chair, and instead, he said, "Trust."

"You trust my nephew, Sairis?"

"I do." He felt nervous saying it, as though he were making himself vulnerable somehow.

But Jessup nodded, a thoughtful expression on his face. "You will not go wrong in that. He is a trustworthy person."

"I know," whispered Sairis and realized more emotion had leaked into his voice than was quite proper. He couldn't bring himself to continue meeting Jessup's gaze and his eyes flicked absently around the table. He caught Quintin staring at him with an expression of pure malice. The man didn't look away as their eyes met and Sairis was forced to break first in order to return polite attention to the commander.

"Sir, how long will we be in this fort?" He hadn't meant to be so blunt, but the words tumbled out. *How long until I'm not trapped in a stone warren with people who hate me? How long until this battle replenishes my magic? How long until I can see Roland again?*

"About five more hours," said Jessup. "If you're finished eating, you should try to sleep." He turned to say something to one of the border lords, and Marsden leaned over to murmur in Sairis's ear, "You're better at making friends than you thought, eh?"

Sairis turned to him with a furious scowl. "I wish you would help me!" he hissed.

"Nonsense. You're doing fine."

"Lord Marsden," called someone from the door, "we've set up wards around the fort, but we were hoping you'd check our work."

Marsden rose, along with several of the other magicians. "Of course."

Sairis returned his attention to his food. Carafes of water and weak wine were coming around, along with plates of chicken. His hunger was still clamoring, and so he ate and listened to Jessup try to soothe the fractious border lords, and when he'd had enough of both, he went to bed.

Potions

S airis woke from a dead sleep to someone shaking him. "Magus Sairis, the commander requires your presence. Get up at once and come with us."

Sairis felt foggy. He couldn't remember where he was for a moment. "Wha—?"

"Now, sir!"

Recollections of the fort and the previous evening stirred as the soldiers—there were three of them—dragged him upright. Sairis had expected to be tired this morning, but he hadn't expected quite such malaise. *Did I not have enough magic to heal myself properly?* His muscles didn't feel sore, though, only his brain.

As he slipped his glasses onto his nose, he was chagrined to see that all three men had crowded into his small room and were standing around him in his shirt and underclothes. Sairis struggled into his trousers while they waited impatiently. "What time is it?" He was growing increasingly certain that he had not slept four or five hours. *One or two at most.*

The guards didn't answer. "No need for a waistcoat," growled one. "Let's go."

He barely managed to snatch his overcoat as they hustled him out the door. *These hallways are cold, damnit!* "Am I in some kind of trouble?" ventured Sairis. He didn't recognize the soldiers. They weren't dressed like scouts, but like the troops from the border lords.

"The lord commander needs a word with you," was all their leader said.

Sairis wished he could wake up. *Am I being abducted again?* They marched him up the stairs, higher into one of the tunneled towers until it dead-ended in a heavy door. The soldiers opened it and pushed Sairis through without announcement. Alarm bells were clanging in his head now, and he was genuinely surprised to find himself in an ordinary study and not some kind of torture chamber.

He saw a desk, rows of books, an intimate dining area with only three chairs and the remains of a tea service. There was no light in the room, but soft lamplight streamed from the far door. "Hello?" ventured Sairis. "Commander Jessup?"

He thought he heard a muffled response. Sairis took a deep breath, tried to force clarity into his foggy head, and went through. The bedchamber looked aggressively martial—weapons on the walls, a map over the fireplace. The lit lamp stood near the bed. Commander Jessup sat on the edge, shoulders slumped, head bowed.

"Sir!" Sairis ran to him, all thoughts of a trap forgotten. "Sir, are you alright?"

The man looked like he'd aged ten years since dinner. He raised vacant eyes to Sairis. His lips moved, but only a garbled hiss emerged. *Fuck!* This looked like the sort of fit elderly men sometimes suffered under stress.

Sairis heartily regretted using the last of his magic to heal sore muscles. The commander might not respond to magical aid. Many mundanes didn't. However, Sairis could have used magic to figure out what was wrong with him. *Did he call for my help, thinking I'm the most powerful magician here?* "Sir, I am so sorry, but I am no good for this. We need Lord Marsden. Or maybe one of his acolytes. I am not a healer. Gods, sir, please lie down. I will get help. I—"

Some flailing part of Sairis's brain threw up the information that Jessup believed Sairis to be collared. *He wouldn't have called for me.*

Oh... Oh, gods, I am slow.

Sairis straightened, and the room rocked. He knew then that what was wrong with the commander was also wrong with him. "Poison." He tried to speak the word aloud, and heard himself slur.

Jessup looked up at him, and Sairis thought his eyes focused for a moment. "We've been poisoned, sir," said Sairis, but it came out distorted and thick.

Need to get Marsden. Need to... Sairis stumbled towards the study, but the room seemed to have gotten a great deal larger. Sairis slumped to his knees long before he reached the door. How had he been able to walk up the stairs? Why was his reaction getting so much worse so fast?

Because it's not poison, whispered a voice that sounded almost like the steady murmur of his teacher. *This is a spell.*

Quintin's icy glare floated before his mind's eye. *"He specializes in potions."*

Sairis remembered how Marsden had been called away to survey the fort's wards just as the last course of food and drink came around. He'd taken his best students with him. *Marsden might have sensed the spell. They didn't think I would because of the collar. And I didn't…because I'd used up the last of my magic.*

Sairis was not a potions master. Neither was Karkaroth. It was an art he knew little about, but he did know that potions could be activated at a distance, provided the victim swallowed the right spelled substances. *The spell's creator activated it right before those men woke me. It was just starting to take hold.*

"My Lord Winthrop has plans for you."

Gods below. He was so cocky. Why didn't I see this coming?

Sairis dredged up every ounce of magic in his system and directed it at his own health. Wards flickered weakly over his skin. His head cleared a trifle, but he could tell he was not winning. Behind him, he heard a thump and turned to see Lord Jessup sprawled on the floor beside his bed.

Sairis crawled to the man and rolled him over. His eyes were glazed and staring, his breath a rattle. Sairis's own chest felt heavy.

On the bedside table, the lamp exploded. Sairis watched, his brain too foggy to fully process what he was seeing, as flames caught in the bedsheets. *The room is on fire,* some part of his brain informed him, *but the poison will kill me first.*

No, whispered the low, implacable voice of Karkaroth. *It will not. Because you are not collared, and you are about to come into some power.*

Then Jessup Malconwy died.

9

Confession

Roland stood with Daphne and Anton at the peak of the North Rim Fort in the chilly stillness of three in the morning and attempted to explain to them what they were seeing in the dark valley below. "This is the narrowest point of the pass—only about forty feet wide. It's the only place really suited to bringing in wagons, supplies, and horses." Roland gestured to the ten-foot stone and stake wall that ran between the forts, delineated by the customary number of nighttime torches. "The wall has been destroyed or damaged many times, but always at great cost to our enemy. He's never managed to penetrate much beyond it. The pass remains narrow for about a quarter mile beyond the wall, as you saw when we came in. Enemy troops are totally exposed in there, and we've prepared every ledge and crevice to rain death from above. It's a tough problem, even for a sorcerer. In four years, he hasn't cracked it, even when he outnumbers us four to one."

Anton nodded. Roland couldn't see their faces, as lights in the fort were being kept to a minimum to avoid arousing suspicion. They'd all had about four hours of sleep, having arrived just after sunset. Daphne and Anton were sipping strong tea, but Roland didn't want it. Tea would only make his nerves jangle. He was wide-awake with that piercing alertness that occurred before a battle.

Anton gestured to the mountains that towered to the north and south. "And there really is no other passage in either direction?"

"No good one. Mount Cairn to the south has seen more skirmishes than any spot apart from the pass itself. It has a number of small ravines, including the Valley of False Hope. However, it's very difficult to bring in supplies. Hastafel's troops run out of food and they have to turn back. The mountain to the north, the one we call The Sentinel, is completely impassable, but we have a watchtower up there that often catches his troop movements in time to give a warning."

"He is, of course, reinforced by sea as long as he stays on the shore," murmured Anton.

"Correct," said Roland with a grimace. "And we receive food and supplies by land. The drought has weakened us, while he never seems to have difficulty bringing in ships."

"The pass gets wider quickly," observed Daphne, straining her eyes towards the mouth of the valley and the sea.

Roland nodded. "In tight spaces, his numbers don't mean much. His troops still have to come at us a few at a time. But as we advance away from the tight walls of this pass, his numbers start to tell. It's a big, open valley out there—about a mile to the ocean. He's been trying to get us to come out for a real fight from the beginning."

They were all silent a moment, watching the distant torches in Hastafel's camp. The sparkle of the sea looked incredibly close beyond the walls of the pass.

"Where does the Valley of False Hope emerge?" asked Daphne.

Roland pointed at a well-known constellation. "You see the Narwhal's Horn?"

Daphne found the star.

"Look straight down from that. There's a saddle up there on Mount Cairn. The path from the valley comes right over the saddle and then down a series of switchbacks."

"Won't Hastafel see the border lords coming, then?" asked Anton.

Roland shook his head. "The peak and the saddle are usually obscured by clouds and rain. It rains excessively on this side of the mountains, the more so the higher you go."

"That's the rain that used to fall on our crops," said Daphne bitterly.

Roland nodded. "It all gets dumped here as the clouds rise up the mountains from the sea. The constant fog and mud are one of the reasons that so many have died up there. That mountain would be hazardous for a pleasure stroll, let alone a troop action."

Anton laughed uneasily.

"Skirmishes occur at times and in places where neither side intended," said Roland. "The deadliest fights in this war have happened on Mount Cairn in deep mud."

"I can see why Mistala has been preoccupied the last few years," said Anton. "I'm impressed that you've held out this long."

Roland said nothing. He was suddenly conscious that Anton was a foreign prince whose forefathers had frequently challenged Mistala's northern border and who would surely have salivated at the details of their neighbor's distress.

Anton seemed to sense Roland's uncertainty, because he added, "Do you know why my father didn't attend our historic meeting, Roland?"

"I assume he did not wish to encounter King Norres," said Roland.

Anton barked a laugh. "Gods, that's reason enough. They would have been dueling in the courtyard a decade ago. But, no. My father did not attend because he is…forgetting things. Names, places, dates… My mother has tried to hide it from the court, but…it is getting worse."

"Oh." Roland wasn't sure what to say. *A secret in exchange for a secret. And yours might actually be bigger.*

Roland reached out in the dark and put a hand on his future brother-in-law's shoulder. "We are fortunate to have you for a friend, Your Highness."

He could hear the smile in Daphne's voice in the darkness. "I told you I have good taste."

"I told you *I* do," said Roland, forgetting to be discreet.

Daphne sighed. "Yes, I hope you're right, and that yours isn't setting Uncle Winthrop on fire right now, for all he deserves it. Now let's go down there and finish a war."

* * * *

Sairis's brain cleared as the magic hit him. A human death right under his hands, and a name he knew.

Sairis lunged for one of the pikes on the wall and stabbed his own finger. He returned to the body and forced his blood through the dead man's half open mouth and onto his tongue. Sairis spoke furiously, the spell stinging his lips as he poured more power than he could afford into one desperate binding. He wished he knew Jessup's middle name. Still, maybe...

Sairis felt the hard tug on his magic that meant he'd succeeded. Jessup Malconwy's ghost had not had time to flee. Like the mouse in the Knave, it had been arrested, bound, though Sairis had no mirror or other device to make it visible. Sairis wrote a rune in blood on the man's forehead and waited. One heartbeat. Two.

Jessup's eyes opened.

"Sir, you are dead," said Sairis quickly. "We were poisoned, and I believe it was by a spell. I have bound your ghost to your body, but I must tell you that this rarely results in a return to life. For any chance of such a thing, we need a physician at once and probably more magicians, too, and I am terribly afraid that we will get neither because there is a military coup going on outside. Also, sir, your room is on fire. Someone spelled your lamp."

Sairis hesitated and then added, "That at least I can do something about." He put a hand on the bedframe and drew the heat—slowly, so as not to burn himself. It was harder than it should have been. Binding the ghost had taken a lot, and he was uncomfortably aware of Quintin's spell, still gnawing inside him.

Jessup looked up at Sairis. He gave a slow blink, as though experimenting with how eyeballs worked. He made a visible effort to draw air into his lungs—a jerky, unnatural movement. "Dead," he repeated. "Yes...I...feel it."

"You won't be able to talk for long," said Sairis. "Sir, I am so sorry, but can you tell me anything about the people who did this to you? Do you have an idea of what is going on? How can I help Roland and Daphne now?"

"My brother," said the ghost dully. "I was afraid he might delay...might avoid arriving at the pass in time. But I never thought he'd do this. I thought we were...better friends than that."

Sairis swallowed a bitter retort. "How does he expect to get away with killing you? Will the border lords really sanction this?"

Jessup's dead face attempted to rearrange itself into a smile. The result was ghastly. "My dear boy, you melted your collar and set his camp on fire once. Do you really think anyone will doubt that you have done it again?"

Sairis felt cold.

"The fort will burn," continued Jessup in a rasp, "because we trusted a necromancer, who'd already gotten loose once. The border lords will arrive to crush Hastafel's weakened army, but not in time to save my niece and nephew. All of this will be blamed on you."

Sairis couldn't breathe. He stared at Jessup's graying face. The corpse could not twist its features into a human expression of comfort, although he thought it tried. Jessup's voice murmured on, "I am certain that my brother is not injured. He will say that he wisely gave an excuse not to come to the fort because he feared your treachery. He will be proven correct, and the lords who were wavering will throw their whole support behind him. Daphne's decision to trust you will be shown to be the sentimentality of women. Winthrop will inherit the throne, and if you somehow escape tonight, he will solidify his position by hunting you down and executing you for, among other things, the death of the man you love."

A tear ran down Sairis's nose and splashed onto Jessup's pallid skin.

"You *are* Roland's lover, aren't you?"

Sairis nodded. He drew a sharp breath and said, "I will not let this happen. My collar is an illusion, as you may have guessed by the fact that I bound you. Now tell me how to get out. There must be more than one exit from this warren. How do I get to the stables without being caught?"

Another slow blink. The ghost was having increasing difficulty with fine movements of the mouth and lips.

"Lord Jessup," said Sairis gently. "I will let you go. I will not keep you here. But I need all the help I can get if I'm going to save Roland and Daphne."

One of the dead man's hands scrabbled awkwardly on the floor. If Sairis had not had extensive experience with corpses, he might have jumped. Instead, he reached out and took the clammy fingers. Sairis realized then that the ghost was not hesitating out of difficulty with speech, but for some other reason. "I believe you may...succeed," he said at last. "In that case, there is something I need to tell Roland. Something for which he may never forgive me."

Oh.

Sairis thought he might know what was coming. "Is this about Marcus?"

The corpse gave a jerk. "You know."

"I know Roland loved him. I know that when I was in Winthrop's camp, his lordship told me that he knew of my relationship with Roland. He tried to threaten me into becoming his spy. He insinuated that he had something to do with Marcus's death." Sairis hesitated. "I did not tell Roland. He has had enough of grief and betrayal lately, and I had no proof."

"Marcus was a ward," murmured Jessup's ghost, "a hostage to his father's good behavior. His father had given trouble before, and Winthrop had had to deal with him. So it seemed plausible when he sent word that he had evidence of Marcus insinuating himself into Roland's affections in order to gather intelligence for his father, who was plotting a rebellion. He said he was sending a man to 'deal' with it. He also pointed out that Roland's 'flaws' made him vulnerable to such schemes."

Sairis listened in silence, sensing the ghost's need to confess and yet wishing he didn't have to hear it.

"I knew of my nephew's proclivities, of course," continued Jessup. "Such secrets don't keep in a close barracks. But men long away from their families have had such attachments since time immemorial, and I saw no harm in it. Marcus was a good soldier, a little uncouth, but smart and brisk about his business. I did not want to believe ill of him, but my brother had been dealing with his father for a long time, and Roland can be... overly trusting...with those he loves.

"Winthrop's man arrived and posed as a recruit. I thought he intended to speak to Marcus before doing anything rash. Within days, the boy was dead. It happened during a chaotic encounter with enemy forces on Mount Cairn. Roland was devastated, but not suspicious. My brother's man went through Marcus's belongings before I thought to have a look at them. He burned all the papers and left the next day. Marcus wasn't a fool. I made a careful inspection of his bunk and found a few letters hidden inside the mattress. They were unsigned, but… my brother's hand is distinctive, and he could not entrust such missives to a secretary."

The ghost's voice was fading, rasping so much that Sairis could barely understand him. "Do you have the letters?" he asked with a mixture of hope and foreboding.

"Inner shirt pocket," gasped Jessup.

Sairis unbuttoned the shirt and located a few pieces of folded paper, still warm from the man's cooling skin. *How long have you slept with your guilt over your heart?* thought Sairis. *About a year, I guess.* "Did Winthrop know you had them?"

"I think he…suspected."

Of course he did. These were probably your death warrant.

Sairis tucked the papers away. A sudden banging on the door made him jump. "My Lord Commander! Is everything alright in there?"

These people are meant to discover my treachery, thought Sairis. *Am I intended to have succumbed to my own fire?*

"My lord, I repeat, is there a way out apart from the main door?"

The ghost was drifting. His sense of guilt had probably been holding him here as much as Sairis's binding and with his confession made, his spirit wanted to fly. "I remember a River," he whispered.

"Yes, I'll put you in it," said Sairis. "Tell me how to get out."

"It was so beautiful," slurred the ghost. "I never knew... I never knew death could be beautiful. I felt so free..."

"Sir, I will never be able to show these letters to Roland if you don't tell me how to leave."

The door in the next room boomed open and footsteps pounded through the study. *Bollocks.* Here he knelt beside Jessup's undead corpse with a blood rune on its forehead. *I am really making this too easy for them.*

Sairis drew on all his remaining magic and hurled a fireball at the tapestry over the door to the study. It burst into flames, along with the rug and part of the wall. The man who'd been in the act of stepping through reeled back.

If I'm to be blamed for setting fires, I might as well set them as I please, thought Sairis.

The bellows of the men in the study were so loud that Sairis almost missed Jessup's whispered words, "Turn the sword to six o'clock."

Sairis looked around wildly. The walls contained all kinds of weapons, but only one sword. Sairis stood up. His necromantic fire burned hotter than ordinary flames. It had already nipped into the study with all those books, and the soldiers were trying desperately to beat it out.

He looked down at Jessup Malconwy's corpse. Its glassy eyes seemed to plead with him. *I could order you to rise and attack those men. A burning corpse stumbling down the stairs... That would certainly make my escape easier. I could leave you bound here to haunt this fort forever, brooding on what you did to a 'good soldier' and your 'trusting' nephew.* But Sairis couldn't bring himself to do it. "Last question," he whispered. "Did you recognize the man your brother sent to kill Marcus?"

Jessup's throat worked as he tried to swallow and couldn't. His breath hissed as he dragged air into his lungs. "Never...seen him before...or since."

Sairis nodded. *Maybe Winthrop disposed of him. Or kept him far away. Or maybe...* Aloud, he said, "Be free," and spoke the rune that would break the binding.

Jessup's eyes grew instantly vacant. The tortured movement of his chest stilled. Sairis hurried towards the sword in the increasingly bright and smoky room, hoping that he really did understand how the hidden exit worked. The weapon rotated easily, and a door opened in the wall, leading to a dark staircase. Sairis looked back once at the still form of Jessup Malconwy.

You fought hard for years, old man, and then you trusted your brother, which should not have been a terrible mistake. I hope that whatever lies beyond the Black Gate treats you kindly.

10

The Advantages and Disadvantages of Living Horses

Daphne insisted on riding with the troops. She would stay in the rear, where she could watch the battle and make decisions, but she would not remain in the fort. She had half a dozen royal guards and they were very good. Roland had put them through their paces himself. Still, he didn't like it. "Daphne, if something goes wrong, we could easily be cut off from the fort. Out there in open ground, outnumbered more than three to one, we'd be slaughtered. A dead queen will do Mistala no good."

"And a live queen who hides in forts will never hold the Mistalan throne," said Daphne as they sat on their horses, watching soldiers march through the heavy northern gate. "You know Uncle Winthrop was only echoing the sort of nonsense the border lords are saying, Roland. The men have to believe in me. If we win this war properly, I do not think we will have a repetition of the sort of treason he was spouting at me in the tent. I believe that all of us want Mistala to prosper, and if I give them what no king has given them, they will bend the knee in earnest. But I have to earn it. I recognize that."

Roland's gauntleted hands shifted around his helm, still in his lap. He thought it was good for the men to see his face before a battle—to see that he was not afraid. Or at least that he did not look it.

"And the other things he said…"

"About you?"

Roland nodded.

Daphne tossed her hair. "If I know you, you'll be on the front lines. You'll be a hero of the war that freed Mistala from a dark sorcerer. No one will dare speak ill of you after today."

He wasn't exactly speaking ill of me, thought Roland. *He was speaking the truth—a truth that can be used as a weapon whenever anyone wants to threaten either of us.*

He shook his head and focused upon the immediate future. *We are about to kick a hornet's nest. Uncle Jessup will be coming over that saddle in a couple of hours, along with Uncle Winthrop and more men than we've ever been able to throw at Hastafel's army. By then, I expect I will be glad to see them, no matter what they think of me.*

* * * *

Sairis was halfway down the long, dark staircase when the weakness hit him so hard he stumbled. *Godsdamn it!* He didn't have enough magic left to purge Quintin's spell from his system. Quintin must realize that things in the tower had not gone according to plan and now he was renewing his attack.

Sairis wondered where Marsden was. *They don't trust him or they wouldn't have gotten him out of the way to set their trap.* Sairis hoped Marsden had gotten wind of the trouble before it started. The idea of the old man knocked on the head sent a curious pang through him. *If he'd put a real collar on me, I'd be dead right now.*

Sairis turned his attention to dismantling Quintin's spell, but it was annoyingly persistent. He needed light and supplies and time. Instead, he was running down stairs in the dark.

Sairis reached the bottom and groped blindly for a door. He found it at last, lifted the dead bolt, and opened it a crack. He was looking at the main courtyard and gate. *So much for a second exit.* The stable entrance was about ten yards away. People were shouting inside the fort, but there didn't seem to be much chaos outside it yet. A steady patter of cold rain looked as though it had been falling for hours, making puddles in the courtyard, filling the air with fine mist. The stables looked quiet in the gray haze.

Sairis wished fervently for his bone charm. Making himself invisible without preparation required an enormous amount of magic that he did not have. *At least the rain and mist will help.* He tried not to think about riding through such weather in the cold dark without a waterproof cloak. *One thing at a time.*

Sairis pushed open the door and walked briskly through the wet, chilly air. *Don't run. Behave as though you belong here.* No one shouted at him to stop, and he encountered no guard at the stable entrance. Sairis wasn't sure what to make of this, but dipped gratefully into the dry, dim interior, redolent of hay and horse. He ran lightly along the row of stalls until he came to the spot where he'd left Butterball a few hours ago.

Sairis stepped into the stall. And stopped. His little horse lay crumpled on the ground. *Oh, no.* Sairis had a brief urge to drop to his knees beside Butterball's head and weep. He was surprised at the strength of his own reaction, considering dead horses really were so much easier.

However, as he leaned over Butterball, he felt a new sense of alarm. The animal was not dead, but sleeping. Drugged or spelled, it made little difference which. Sairis could raise a dead horse, but there wasn't much he could do with a sleeping one.

And somebody knew that.

"Well, you're just as much trouble as I expected."

Sairis spun around. Quintin was standing in the door to the stall. He wore a cloak with the cowl pulled up, but Sairis recognized his voice. "Everybody says necromancers are hard to kill. Even Hastafel had a go at you and missed, didn't he?"

"Actually, he didn't miss," said Sairis, his mouth running away with his brain as he tried to think of a way to escape. "He put a sword through me. Or his demon did."

Quintin took a step forward.

Sairis leapt for the side of the stall. He wasn't much of a climber, but in his fear he nearly made it over the top before Quintin got a handful of his clothes and yanked him down hard into the straw and dirt. Sairis drew on every bit of magic he possessed and spoke a rune that he'd only used once in his life—knowledge dearly won from a book that ought to have been burned.

Quintin gasped and stumbled against the wooden wall of the box. For one instant, his ghost became visible as a mist in the air. Sairis was peeling it from his body as a person might peel a fruit. Quintin screamed. Somewhere further down the line of stalls, a horse gave an answering neigh and there was a crash.

Then Sairis lost the thread of his spell. His body folded against the ground and he crouched there struggling to breathe. He could hear Quintin's panting as the other magician straightened. Quintin's shadow fell across Sairis in the dim light from the stable door. The toe of his boot caught Sairis hard in the stomach and flipped him onto his side. Sairis tasted blood and not just from the kick. The spell he'd tried to use was nasty, but he was desperate. And it hadn't even worked. *I don't know his true name, and he's got his magic inside me.*

Quintin leaned over, grabbed Sairis by the hair, and dragged him to his knees. "You absolute shit," he spat. "Did Marsden fuck up your collar on purpose or by accident? Well, it doesn't matter." He forced something into Sairis's mouth—something that tasted of iron.

Sairis thrashed, his fear giving way to blind panic. The object seared his throat and tongue. It was bad, bad, very bad...

Quintin pinned him down easily in his weakened state and held his mouth shut. As the bite of the spelled iron slid down Sairis's throat, Quintin leaned close and whispered. "That's going to kill you, mate. And I'm going to have a bit of fun while you're dying. A necromancer on his knees, eh? Couldn't pass that up. And a prince's leavings besides. I figure his highness owes me, what with me cleaning up after him all the time."

Potions can alter appearances. "You killed Marcus," whispered Sairis, his lips thick and numb around the words.

"Were you his fuck toy, too? Gods, all you perverts know each other. Now, let's see if I like what princes like while you can still squirm a little."

In his pain and terror, Sairis forced his eyes away from Quintin. *The River, the River, I don't want to stay for this.* But he couldn't find his center.

Something white floated into view over Quintin's shoulder. Quintin slapped at it with his free hand. "Bugger off, horse."

The horse opened its mouth and bit him.

11

The Battle is Joined

S unrise was still two hours off when the foremost of Daphne's troops encountered the first line of real pickets. The fight in complete darkness was short and brutal. Roland was in the thick of it. No one escaped.

However, the next picket was larger. These men had obviously heard the commotion and were better prepared. The thump of vanishing hoofbeats echoed through the night even before Roland's men had fully engaged. *That will be a runner sent to sound the alarm.*

As swords clanged in the pre-dawn glow, Roland caught a rumble from the direction of the sea. Torches blazed through distant shadows. Something howled in the night, the eerie sound floating across the valley.

Well, I believe we've got his attention, thought Roland. *Here come the hornets.*

* * * *

Quintin made an animal scream, muffled because the horse's blunt teeth were encompassing his entire nose and most of one cheek. The scream broke into a wheezing gurgle as the animal jerked back. The mask of blood that had become Quintin's head lurched in the other direction.

Sairis stared up at the nightmare of a horse, holding a man's face between its teeth. "Cato?"

Quintin was still howling, but that didn't last long. One of Cato's hooves lashed out and caught the blinded man in the shoulder, bringing him down hard into the straw. One more kick and he lay still.

The spell shattered.

Sairis felt the jolt of the recoil. He'd still swallowed a scrap of poisonous iron, but the deadly focus of the magic that had been spreading through his entrails died along with its maker. *I might live.*

The iron, however, was still soaking up every bit of magic he might have gained from Quintin's death. Sairis tried to stand and staggered against the wall of the box. Cato's head arched towards him and Sairis flinched away. There was nowhere to run. *One kick is all it would take. Or is he going to tear my face off, too?* The horse nickered beside his ear. Something brushed Sairis's cheek like wet velvet. No teeth.

Sairis opened his eyes and stared into the black gaze of Roland's destrier, at the snowy muzzle slick with blood. "Did four days of riding make us friends, Cato?"

Apparently it had.

Sairis patted Cato's neck—gingerly at first, with hands that shook. "Good horse," he whispered. He repeated it mindlessly over and over. "Good horse, good horse." He was shaking all over now. *I have to get out of here.*

But he could barely stand. More noise was coming from the fort—sounds of fighting, confused and muted through the drumming of the rain.

He glanced at Quintin's corpse. He heartily wished he could send it walking through the fort, preferably on fire. But he didn't have the magic, nor did he truly have the will to chase down Quintin's ghost in the River without knowing its true name. He was a little afraid even to go poking through the pockets, since the man obviously kept poisonous spells, and Sairis did not have the training to recognize or use them. In the end, Sairis only took Quintin's cloak. It looked waterproof, and it swallowed his smaller frame. With the hood up, no one would see his face...or the blood that had spattered his clothes.

This done, Sairis limped down the hall to Cato's stall. The stallion had kicked the door hard enough to break the latch. "Good horse," murmured Sairis again. The destrier followed him. Sairis had to force himself not to flinch when the soft nose nibbled at his ear.

"They said you couldn't carry Roland in his armor...but what about me?" Sairis surely weighed nothing by comparison.

It took him two tries to get the saddle over Cato's back. The horse stood patiently while he tightened the girth, cursing his clumsy fingers. Someone burst into the stable while he was working on the bridle. Sairis ducked into the back of Cato's stall, heart in his throat.

Running feet pounded through the stable. A stall door banged, and a horse whinnied. Sairis listened enviously as someone nimbler and more expert than himself saddled a horse at speed and then rode out at a fast clip.

Sairis got to work again. By the time he was done, another man had run in and out with a different horse. No one seemed to have glanced into Butterball's stall. *Hurry, hurry, hurry.*

Cato was so much taller than a pony. Sairis's wobbly legs refused to cooperate as he struggled to reach the stirrup. He ended up climbing the horse with hands and feet in a graceless scramble. Amazingly, Cato stood still for it.

You need to sleep, whispered a voice in Sairis's head. *Heal yourself. You almost died. You're still hurt.*

No.

Exhaustion was a hand on Sairis's shoulders, pushing him down as Cato stepped from the stables. *Do not faint, do not faint...*

Men were fighting in the courtyard. One of the outbuildings was on fire in spite of the rain. Sairis couldn't see very well with his hood up. He sat hunched on Cato's back as the horse moved at an agonizingly unhurried clip-clop through the mud and puddles of the courtyard. Then they were at the gate, and finally someone shouted. "Who goes there?"

Sairis realized he would have to get down to lift the heavy bar. *I'll never make it back up into the saddle.*

Despair washed through him as he stared at the gate. *Some wizard you are. You got all this way, survived two attempts to kill you this evening, and you're going to die because you couldn't open an ordinary gate.*

"I said who are you?" insisted the unfriendly voice, now directly behind him. "Answer me, or I shoot."

The voice broke off with a grunt. Sairis didn't dare turn around to show his face. *I have to get down. I have to try.*

A man's hand closed around Cato's bridle from the side. The horse gave an angry squeal, but the hand held him in place. To Sairis's astonishment, the soldier raised the bar on the gate and pushed it open. Then he stepped aside.

Sairis couldn't help turning to stare at his benefactor. The fellow had his own hood up, but the eyes looking out of the shadows of his cowl were an unnaturally brilliant green.

Sairis gaped. *Mal?*

One green eye winked. Then he gave Cato a slap on the rear that sent the horse trotting down the defile, away from the chaos of the burning fort, towards the valley that was living up to its name.

12

In the Fog

S airis didn't dare urge Cato to gallop. He was uncertain of his ability to stay on a galloping horse at the best of times, much less in his current condition. Soldiers rushed past him. Sairis expected to be accosted at any moment, but apparently Cato's stately plod aroused no suspicion. *At least we don't look like we're fleeing after assassinating the commander.*

The main trail was a confusion of scattered torchlight in the rain. The dust from the day's ride had turned to thick mud.

Sairis turned Cato west along the trail, heading further into the mountains. *What am I doing? Running away from Winthrop? Running towards Roland? Do I think I can redeem this disaster all by myself?*

Maybe, whispered a voice in his head. *Maybe… And anyway, you have to try.*

It wasn't long before he passed the last of the waterlogged men and horses, the last of the torches. The sounds of uproar died away behind him. Sairis was in complete darkness on a steep, mud-slick trail, riding a fickle destrier who could toss him off at a whim.

This is the most ill-advised thing I have ever done in my life. To make matters worse, he was feeling increasingly ill. Quintin's spell had become a diffuse pain in his abdomen, the iron soaking up any magic that might have healed him. Sairis wondered if even human deaths in the nearby fort would provide him with power at this moment. *I've no idea how to treat magical poisoning.*

Cato slipped and Sairis's heart gave a sickening squeeze, but the warhorse righted himself and continued. *Roland spent four years fighting out here, and Cato has been with him the whole time. Cato must know this terrain as well as Roland does. Still, they call this the Valley of False Hope for a reason.*

Weakness came in waves. Sairis leaned over Cato's neck, shivering, unable to see anything in the wet darkness. *Don't faint. Do. Not. Faint.*

He fainted.

* * * *

Roland's initial attack with handpicked cavalry from the fort worked so well that by the time dawn glowed around the horizon, he and his men were perhaps a quarter of a mile from the sea. They'd driven a deep wedge into Hastafel's surprised army, softening the path of the infantry coming behind and creating chaos that Lamont's cavalry could capitalize on, in spite of being less experienced in this terrain.

The risk, of course, was that Roland and his men would drive too deeply into enemy territory and become cut off or overwhelmed. Without light, it had been difficult for Roland to judge the state of the action as a whole, but as the first rays broke over the mountains to the east, he turned in his saddle and saw the pass as it must always look to Hastafel's troops—a long slope that rose up from the sea to a narrow corridor where the dawn was glowing. Roland was at the bottom of the hill now, and there was intense fighting for about half a mile up the valley. It was impossible to see who was winning, but the wave of blue from Lamont's mounted troops was certainly making a dent in Hastafel's southern flank.

Roland spotted one of the golems—a lumbering hill of mud. He heard the insane battle-cry of Hastafel's troops, a sort of human wolf-howl that made his skin prickle. Roland had hoped that, in addition to softening the enemy, his vanguard action would draw the worst of the monsters to the most experienced knights from the fort. *If anyone knows how to deal with them, we do.* But the handful of golems had remained out of sight or far away on the horizon.

And we're out of time for this. Hastafel's troops were organizing, closing up behind Roland and his men. *It's now or never if we want to make it back to the rest of the army.* "Fall back!" he bellowed.

The first surprise was over. The second would not be along for an hour or more. *Time for some hard fighting.*

* * * *

Sairis rode through a gray world of swirling mist. He thought it was the banks of the Styx. He could hear water not far off. But that didn't seem right. He'd never encountered such fog on the Styx. He could barely make out the ears of his horse.

Which shouldn't exist, now that he thought about it. He'd never had a horse on the Styx, either.

Sairis thought perhaps he was in the mirror maze. This seemed like one of those in-between places.

Gradually, he became aware that someone was riding beside him. The stranger was dressed like a cavalry officer, with the full beard of a man who had been living in the wilderness for some time. Sairis noticed that in spite of the man's easy movement on the horse's back, his tack and bridle made not a rustle or a clink. Sairis could hear his own horse's footfalls and breathing, but his companion's animal walked as silently as a great cat.

"Who are you?" whispered Sairis, but the man did not turn to look at him.

Something stirred in the fog to his left. Sairis turned and saw another figure, this one surely no older than himself. The fellow was jogging in full military gear, his light armor bumping against his body, a sword slung over his back. And yet his movements made no noise. Beyond him, Sairis caught sight of another horse and rider, more men on foot, more horses... There were hundreds of them, perhaps thousands, moving through the fog.

I need magic, thought Sairis. *I need blood or names or...* "Who are you?" he demanded. "Tell me, so that I can help you."

The man riding beside him turned, and his eyes were not friendly. "Who are *you?*"

* * * *

Sairis came to, slumped over Cato's neck. The horse had stopped walking. The sky overhead was pearl gray through the heavy clouds, though Sairis could see little beneath the trees around him. The world was quiet, except for the steady patter of rain.

Dawn. The reality cut through Sairis's confused thoughts. *It's dawn, and Roland and Daphne and Anton and all their men are fighting for their lives in the valley, expecting reinforcements at any moment…*

Sairis risked a kick to Cato's flanks. The horse gave a grumbling whinny. He took a few more steps and then subsided. Sairis gritted his teeth. He managed to get one rubbery leg over the saddle and slid to the ground. His boots squelched into mud, but at least Roland had gotten him good ones and they weren't sucked off his feet. Sairis held Cato's reins in the white-knuckled grip of a person who thinks he may fall from a mountain at any moment, and cautiously advanced.

There was a tree down across the path. From the ground, Sairis could see better. He realized, with a stab of hope, that they were no longer on the side of the cliff. *Cato brought me to the top of the ridge.*

"Good horse," whispered Sairis. "Good horse, good horse…"

In order to get around the fallen tree, they had to make a detour through brambles. Sairis wished he had been allowed to put on his waistcoat, if only for another layer of fabric between his skin and the vicious thorns. He slipped twice and came up muddy and bleeding. Cato endured the thorns with remarkably good grace, though he did balk when Sairis tried to drag him through a tight space beneath another fallen tree.

By the time they made it back onto the path again, there was enough light to see the trail even from Cato's saddle. *Hurry,* thought Sairis. *Hurry, hurry!* He wished he'd paid more attention at the commander's table last night when men were talking about landmarks. The woods on top of the saddle of Mount

Cairn were as dense as a jungle. Sairis had never seen so much green in all his life. *Is this what it looks like when a forest gets rain?*

Sairis had to climb down from the saddle over and over to navigate around fallen trees. Each time, he thought he might not make it back up. He could tell that his magic had neutralized a bit of the iron. *But not nearly enough.*

A fine, swirling mist joined the bands of rain. *We're in a cloud,* thought Sairis. *Surely that means we're near the top.* The trail had turned to a torrent of gushing mud. It narrowed and narrowed. Then, it disappeared.

* * * *

Roland's men encountered the first golem about halfway back to the main army. This one had a number of human skulls half-buried in the mud of its vaguely humanoid body. Its many mouths went *click, click, click!* It cried out at random in the voices of dead men.

"Sir!" shouted an officer at Roland's elbow, and Roland realized he had stopped moving.

Roland took a deep breath, shook sweat out of his eyes, and reached for his lance. "Distance weapons!" he bellowed. "Take it apart! Do not listen to anything it says! It is not alive! It is not human!"

In the background, he could hear the thing weeping for its mother. At the same time, its great clay fist flew out with unexpected speed and knocked a man from his horse. Fortunately, his companions reacted quickly. By the time Roland's men had managed to disassemble the monster they were in the thick of the fighting, dodging pikes and arrows from Hastafel's troops as well as grappling with the golem.

Roland had lost good men already, and the battle was just getting started. He couldn't help a glance to the south. The saddle of Mount Cairn was predictably obscured by cloud. *Come on, Uncle Jessup. We need you now.*

* * * *

At first, Sairis didn't panic. The trail had been faint at times before. However, as he searched further and further afield with no sign of a path in the dense foliage, he began to lose his nerve. *What if it's been completely washed away? What if I lost it a long time ago? What if I've been following a game trail or mud run-off all morning?* The sun was well up now, though it rarely appeared through the rain and mist.

At last, Sairis gave up searching for the trail and just moved due north, keeping the morning light on his right shoulder, leading Cato. He came out abruptly on the brink of gray nothingness. Sairis leaned out cautiously, trying to gauge the height of the slope. It might have been a cliff or a ditch for all he could tell in the rolling clouds. He took a few experimental steps down the steep incline, but Cato flatly refused to follow, and he was forced to come back up.

Well, I can't go north any longer. He turned and walked west along the edge of the gray expanse.

He'd been walking for a little while when the clouds opened abruptly, and Sairis took a startled step farther from the edge. The ground was a *long* way down. Sairis's eyes were drawn inexorably westward to that blue that he'd seen only once in a fragment of memory inside Hastafel's sword.

The Shattered Sea. His eyes skipped back to the valley below him. *That's got to be the pass.* People moved like ants over the valley floor. *Daphne's troops were wearing green. Lamont's were wearing blue. Hastafel's men wear a lot of brown and gray.* The green was hard to see, as Sairis was sure soldiers from the pass intended. However, the flash of knightly armor could not be mistaken. *One of those specks is Roland.* The knights were spread out over the valley, fanning out from the pass. The blue line was cutting through Hastafel's flank on the same side as Mount Cairn.

From up here, Sairis could see something else: troops moving along the northern edge of the valley, almost indistinguishable from the rocks. *They're trying to cut our soldiers off from the fort,* Sairis realized. And there were so many more of them. It was obvious from such a bird's eye view. *Roland needs help now.*

Sairis struggled back into Cato's saddle and directed him west along the cliff. He dared to give the horse a kick and gritted his teeth as Cato picked up his pace. *The trail must go down the cliff near here. I can't be that far from it. All I have to do is keep moving along the edge until I find where the trail descends. Then, if I can get a little lower, a little closer to the battle, surely I'll have all the magic a necromancer could ever want.*

13

Flanked

There came a point in any intense action when Roland lost sight of the bigger picture. It was one disadvantage of being the sort of leader people called "hero"—the sort who rode in front and led by example. Roland couldn't worry about whether Lamont had broken through Hastafel's southern flank or whether Daphne was staying safely out of the front lines or whether they were overextending themselves to the south. He couldn't even worry about how many men he'd lost, or whether his company was sticking together or whether the wounded he'd sent to the rear had made it safely out of the fighting. Roland's world shrank to the next man coming at him—men on foot with spears or swords, mounted warriors with lances. His focus dwindled to the space around his horse's head and the increasingly treacherous footing.

And then Roland was glad that he had not taken Cato into this fight, because a crossbow bolt caught his horse in the throat. The bolt penetrated the horse's leather armor and went so deep that Roland saw the tip protruding from the animal's neck.

Then all Roland could think about was falling. Falling and not dying or being pinned or trampled. The horse, at least, did not suffer. It went down so hard and so fast that it didn't have time to roll or kick in its death throes. That probably saved

Roland's life, because the enemies around him did not give him time to recover.

Roland staggered free of his fallen horse and pulled his sword loose just in time to block a pike aimed at his head. A battle axe made a meaty *thunk* as it missed him by inches and slammed into the dead horse. Then one of his men leapt in to engage a rider that would have trampled Roland into the blood-drenched soil. Another of his men, also on foot, turned back-to-back with him and Roland had a moment to catch his breath. All around them the fighting was intense. The ground was spongy with rain and now slick with blood.

A creature came at Roland from around his dead horse. *A man,* he reminded himself, *just a badly injured man.* But the man's face was a bloody pulp on one side. A loop of intestines protruded from an awful stab wound in his abdomen. He should be seeking the rear of his own lines, looking for a doctor and a place to lie down, perhaps a cool drink before he died. Instead, he was roaring like an animal, holding a weapon that looked like a scythe. He should have been weak, but he slammed into Roland with such force that Roland barely kept his footing.

The man didn't stop after Roland cut his legs from under him. He grabbed at Roland's greaves and tried to trip him as another enemy attacked. He was biting the leather of Roland's boots as Roland finally shook him loose.

Roland wanted to shout at him, "Why do you care so much?! This isn't your homeland! What did we ever do to you?"

A voice in his head whispered, *How is this any different from fighting the walking dead? When Hastafel can fill them with this much hate and rage? We need magic. We need...more men.*

Roland sensed that things were not going well. No matter how many enemies he killed, they just kept coming. Rain had begun to sweep across the battlefield, and a wind was blowing from the sea—a strong salt tang that might have been invigorating in other circumstances. But the Shattered Sea was Hastafel's weapon, not Mistala's. It brought him magic and reinforcements.

The sun, when it peeked through the clouds again, was well up the sky. *If we last until midday, we'll be doing better than Uncle Jessup ever expected,* whispered a voice in Roland's mind. *No. Reinforcements will sweep down from Mount Cairn at any moment, and Hastafel will get the surprise of his life.*

"Sir!"

A mounted soldier was trying to approach. He was clearly hesitant to shout Roland's name for fear of making him a priority target. Roland worked his way towards the messenger.

"Sir, your sister would like a word."

Roland looked for his senior lieutenant and was grateful to find him alive. "Noel, take charge. Cover us."

Another downpour of rain swept across the valley as Roland and the messenger worked their way back through the lines. The rain helped to wash some of the mud and ichor from his armor, although it made the ground even more treacherous. As the excitement of battle dissipated, Roland became conscious of the many bruises beneath his steel plates. One of his greaves was missing. The other hung crooked where a strap had been severed, possibly by human teeth. He had a dent so deep in the side of his breastplate that the metal was cutting him. That needed to be hammered out. *And I need a new horse.*

Roland realized that the messenger was leading him, not straight up the valley, but south. He had a terrible suspicion. "Have we been cut off from the forts?"

"I…believe that is a concern, sir," said the soldier miserably.

This was always how it would end without enough men, thought Roland. *This is why Uncle Jessup never allowed himself to be drawn out here.* Roland's eyes strayed to the slopes of Mount Cairn, now directly ahead. Streamers of cloud blew around the summit, which seemed both impossibly close and impossibly far away. Roland strained his eyes for movement in the rain.

* * * *

Sairis urged Cato into a teeth-jarring trot. He was barely staying on, and yet he soon decided that they needed to go faster. His glimpses of the valley were maddeningly brief through the drifting clouds, but he grasped that the bulk of Daphne's army had swung south with Lamont's breaching charge. This had left them thin in the area of the forts.

Sairis didn't know much about war or battles, but he knew about tricks. *There's no more tempting lure than an apparent mistake. If Hastafel let them break his southern lines in order to draw them away from the fort, they won't have enough men to correct the error. They'll be cut off from the fort, from supplies, from their only possible retreat. He'll crush them against Mount Cairn.*

Cato couldn't really gallop, not in the mud and undergrowth, but he opened into a canter that was surprisingly smooth. The wind was coming from the west—salt in the air. Sairis felt as though something inside him was expanding, blossoming in the rain from the Shattered Sea. He felt stronger. But still he found no way to descend the impossibly steep slope.

Perhaps an hour passed, and the terrain grew more broken. Cato could no longer canter. Boulders the size of cottages littered the slope and the clifftop. Sairis was breathing hard. His glasses kept fogging.

At last, a sheer rockface rose out of the mist ahead. Sairis stared at it in bewilderment—forty feet of unscalable cliff. He couldn't continue west without either climbing it, which was impossible, or taking what looked like a very lengthy detour into the dense forest.

Sairis slid off Cato's back. He walked to the rockface and put both hands against it, as though testing to see whether it was real. *No.*

In a burst of frustration, he slammed his fists into the rock and screamed, "No, no, no!" *It can't end here. I will find a way down. I will find a way if I have to teach myself to fly.*

To his right, the mist cleared again, and he saw the wave of gray and brown churning near the tight opening at the top of the valley.

It's already too late, whispered a voice in his head. *It was too late when you failed to save Jessup Malconwy. Did you really think that you constitute reinforcements all by yourself? You have failed. Roland is probably already dead. He died waiting for you. Winthrop will come along later to pick up the pieces. He'll blame you for everything, and won't he be a little bit right after all?*

"No," whispered Sairis. Tears of grief and frustration mingled with the water beading on his cheeks.

It occurred to him that he'd left his tower looking for water, and here it was all around him—the rain stolen by the Sundering, the rain that should have watered Karkaroth's wood, falling here on this accursed mountain. He'd found it, and he could do nothing with it. Nothing to help his master, nothing to help Roland. The source of all magic lay in a vast sparkling swath before his very eyes, and thousands of men were dying below him, and he could do nothing with any of it.

What if I just stepped off the cliff? wondered Sairis. *When I get close enough to the battle, will I have enough magic to cushion my fall?* He'd never heard of such a thing. *But if I fail...I won't know, will I? Not for long.*

Cato gave an uneasy snort and stamped a hoof. Sairis turned sharply, expecting to see the vanguard of Winthrop's soldiers or scouts. But he saw nothing, only the drifting cloud. He noticed that the birds had stopped singing. An instant later, the sun disappeared again. *Then* Sairis saw them.

14

Hungry Ghosts

Roland found Daphne in a stand of trees beside one of the many little rivulets flowing from the mountains. She was surrounded by about two thirds of her original guard. They had clearly seen action. Several were missing pieces of armor. More than one horse was limping. Daphne had intentionally gone into the fight dressed in plain cavalry garb to avoid attracting enemy sharpshooters. She still looked unharmed, though wet and muddy.

She was talking to Anton, who had not been so lucky. A physician stood beside his horse, dressing a wound that had caught him near the knee and must be causing a great deal of pain. Anton's face was pale, but he listened with fierce concentration as Daphne spoke.

"Roland!" she called as soon as she saw him.

Roland strode forward. It was good to see her face, though it looked pinched and anxious. "Daphne!"

He reached up to take her hand in both of his, and then realized his gauntlets were still covered in gore. Daphne hesitated and Roland withdrew his hands quickly. "Pardon. I'll express my affection when I'm not so filthy."

Daphne's eyes raced over him. "Roland, are you hurt?"

"Nothing serious. How bad is our situation?"

Daphne sighed. "Pretty bad. I was so enthusiastic when Hastafel's southern flank broke that we drove too deeply and committed too many troops."

"I did that," said Anton quickly.

"I gave my blessing," said Daphne.

"Pursuing a breaking flank is not normally considered a mistake," said Roland wearily. "I gather we were too thin in front of the fort at that point?"

"He had troops working their way around from the north the entire time," said Daphne. "He drew us away from the fort and then struck. It's the oldest trick imaginable."

"It's a trick that will have cost him many lives," said Roland.

"True," said Anton. "We did make an impact. However, I suspect that without the border lords, we were outnumbered by more than two to one when the fight started. While we've given a good account of ourselves, we have not yet carried the day."

This was an extraordinarily delicate way of saying they were losing. "Has he taken the forts?" said Roland impatiently.

"The Northern Rim for certain," said Daphne. "It is unclear whether he has breached the Southern Rim Fort, but I'm afraid he will do so shortly if I don't pull everyone back to defend it."

Roland screwed his eyes shut. They had started the day with two unbreachable forts and a barricade wall that years of sorcery had been unable to penetrate. Now, they had lost at least one fort and, with it, the integrity of the wall.

And what had they gotten in exchange? *Nothing,* Roland thought miserably. *That was always the gamble.*

"They'll be here soon." The words fell out of his mouth before he could stop them.

Daphne and Anton went still.

"Uncle Jessup…and Sairis. They are coming."

Daphne and Anton glanced at each other sidelong. Roland pounced on the look. "What?" he demanded. "Have you had news of them?"

Daphne shook her head. "I sent a signal to our watch tower on The Sentinel. There was a break in the clouds and enough light for mirrors, so I was able to signal and get a response. They don't see any movement on the saddle, Roland. And they've had some good looks through the rain."

Roland swallowed. "How long ago?"

"About an hour."

"All kinds of things can change in an hour."

"I know!" Daphne's voice broke and Roland felt guilty for pushing her. She'd never seen a battle before, and no matter how cool her mask, it must be a shock. She bore a paralyzing amount of responsibility, and she was trying to make decisions with no good options.

But if there was ever a time when we could not afford to spare each other's feelings, it is now.

"Daphne, if they do not come, we cannot win," he stated bluntly. "Hope is all we have, and I *do* still have it. I do not believe Uncle Jessup or Sairis would abandon us. I do not believe Marsden would. I confess I have doubts about Uncle Winthrop, but we sent him off in good hands. And no matter what else I think of him, I cannot believe he is in bed with Hastafel."

Daphne's face cracked into a laugh that Roland suspected she desperately needed. The idea of his uncle making the two-backed beast with a sorcerer suddenly struck him as absurdly funny, as well. He laughed so hard that it felt like his bruised sides would split open. He looked up to see Anton shaking in his saddle, grimacing and snorting by turns. The pain in his knee was obviously making it difficult to enjoy a joke, but he was trying. *Gods, I wish Sairis were here. I wish we were playing cards in the Tipsy Knave.*

"No," said Daphne, wiping her eyes, "I do not believe Uncle Winthrop has been sending love letters across the barricade. I'm afraid the fate of our reinforcements may be bound up in something more ordinary. Like mud and broken wagons."

"They would still get through on foot," said Roland. "Something must have caused more difficulty than we expected. Probably a landslide. But they will get through."

"Before noon?" asked Anton softly. "Because I'm not sure we've got longer than that."

Roland swallowed. "It does not take long to reach this valley once you start down the slope from the saddle. The first part of the descent begins in a cave. You come out halfway down the cliff, and then the switchbacks are steep. One comes down fast."

"How fast?" pressed Daphne.

"About an hour."

"But that's one man on a fresh horse, right? What about a column of men who have slept little and have been struggling through rain and mud?"

"Maybe two hours," allowed Roland.

"Right." Daphne sat back in her saddle. "So, if Uncle Jessup reached the summit *immediately* after The Sentinel watcher communicated with me, he would still be an hour away. And that's if he appeared at the soonest possible moment."

"Yes," admitted Roland.

A moment of silence, punctuated only by Anton's involuntary gasp as the physician finished the dressing on his leg and carefully placed it back in the stirrup.

"Here is what I am thinking," said Daphne at last. "We cannot let Hastafel have the southern fort. It is our only retreat if things go badly here, and it is Mistala's only defense. Lamont's too. If we are to keep Hastafel from sweeping down on every kingdom east of the Shattered Sea, we cannot lose control of the pass."

"Agreed," said Roland.

"However," continued Daphne. "Right now, we have our backs to Mount Cairn. In order to reach the Southern Rim Fort, we'll need to advance across the valley, and…"

"And we may be surrounded," finished Roland with a chill.

Daphne nodded. "Particularly if he has already taken the Southern Rim, which I cannot rule out at this moment. But I think we must risk it." She smiled with a look of stubborn bravery. "And by the time we reach it…Uncle Jessup will come sweeping down out of the mountains, and that will change everything."

* * * *

Sairis stared at the ghosts of Mount Cairn in the mist. He saw them, not through the fog, but in it. They appeared and disappeared in shreds and streamers.

Sairis had rarely had occasion to fear ghosts on the mortal plane. He was aware, of course, that various factors could cause a spirit to linger. He had dealt with the ghosts of several murder victims when villagers had come to the tower and offered money. But he'd never seen unquiet spirits in such numbers.

No wonder Roland speaks with dread about this mountain. It's haunted.

Sairis wondered whether proximity to the Shattered Sea had anything to do with such a phenomenon. *Probably. We're basically standing in a rain of magic.*

But he couldn't access it.

Even without much power, however, Sairis still had one thing any ghost would like. He searched through the pockets of his coat and found that he still had his little knife. He started to prick his finger and then hesitated. *These are ghosts of Mistala, and Mount Cairn is the biggest boundary stone in existence.*

Sairis found a flat rock. Then he sliced across his palm, the way the kings made their blood oath. Sairis held out his hand and looked at the ghosts as the blood dribbled onto the rock.

They came like crows to offal, crowding around, sipping and lapping greedily. As they drank, their bodies grew more solid, took on traces of color. Sairis could hear them as though at a distance. The officer from Sairis's dream was the first to stand up. Bright eyes flecked with green glittered savagely at Sairis.

"More," he hissed.

"No," said Sairis. "First you will guide me down the mountain."

"More now," murmured another ghost, this one at least six feet tall with a pike the size of a small tree over his shoulder.

"Necromancer," murmured the officer as though the word tasted foul, "we will drain you and leave you like a husk."

"You will not," said Sairis. "Because I can do what no one else can do for you. I can give you rest."

"No rest," snarled the giant with the pike. His face contorted, his jaw opening far wider than any human jaw ought to open. "Vengeance!"

"Vengeance!" shouted the ghosts behind him, their voices like a far-off rustle.

"I can give you that, too," said Sairis. He was starting to sweat, but he knew he must not lose his nerve. Not when dealing with hungry ghosts. He was tempted to try to bind them. They'd taken his blood, and even without their names, he might be able to do it. *But not all of them. I don't have enough blood in my body. Or enough magic.*

Sairis fixed his eyes on the cavalry officer who seemed to be in charge. "Roland and Daphne Malconwy are fighting for their lives down there. I came to save them, but I need your help. I am not going to bind you or compel you. I can't. I am asking."

The ghost stared at him, its expression unreadable. Then it smacked its lips once. "You...taste of...my prince..."

Roland's blood in my wards. Sairis had almost forgotten.

"You have his horse," whispered another ghost.

"Yes," said Sairis faintly. And then, before he thought about it, "I love him."

For a moment, he could hear nothing but the wind and rain in the trees, and he did not know whether he'd said a magic word or pronounced a death sentence. Then the cavalry officer grinned and his lips and teeth were red. "A necromancer asks a favor of a ghost?" he hissed.

"I do," said Sairis faintly.

The officer looked around at the others, then back at Sairis. "And you will give us vengeance upon the sorcerer's hosts?"

"I will," said Sairis. "My blood will only give you voices for a short time, but I will give you the blood of your enemies."

They flickered and twisted in the mist, whispering.

The cavalry officer gave a mad laugh. He jumped onto his shadowy mount and started away at a trot. He didn't say, "This way" or "Follow me." But ghosts were like this. They forgot about human niceties.

Sairis made a desperate scramble onto Cato's back. The horse looked nervous, but not spooked. Sairis doubted he could see the ghosts, although he could probably sense something. The forest was very dark, with no sign of a trail, but Sairis fixed his eyes on the dead cavalry officer and moved through a mist of hungry ghosts into the dripping trees.

15

Drunk on Death

B ugles brayed across the valley, calling Mistalan troops to rejoin the rest of the army beneath Mount Cairn. Roland found a new horse—there were a distressing number available—and put his equipment to rights as much as possible. Then he assisted the officers in making a count, organizing what supplies they had, and bringing physicians to the wounded. Mercifully, Hastafel's men did not press after them, but took the opportunity to regroup and lick their own wounds.

That was the good news. The bad news was that about a third of their troops were dead or missing, and the rain was getting worse. Daphne couldn't tell the state of the Southern Rim Fort because they could not see the flags. Within half an hour, they could not even see the walls. Officers debated the merits of waiting until conditions improved, but Daphne kept shaking her head. "The fort is lightly manned. If our people are fighting to hold it, we must go to their aid. Without the fort, we are lost."

Roland could see in the men's faces that they thought they were lost anyway. They all knew exactly how difficult it would be to retake the Rim Forts, because they'd held them for years.

But Daphne was right. They had to keep behaving as though they had a chance.

As soon as the army had properly regrouped, the forces of Mistala and Lamont advanced from their relatively sheltered position with their backs against the sheer face of Mount Cairn. They encountered less resistance than Roland had expected as they moved through the drenching rain. Archers shot at them, and cavalry harried their flanks, but the fierce fighting did not recommence.

Roland didn't like it. When at last they came within sight of the walls, it became apparent that the flagpoles had been cut down. A long, dripping sash had been flung over the battlements—black as the demon wolf.

Roland felt as though he were moving in a dream. A cold, hard knot formed in his stomach. The men behind him expressed their despair openly. "The fort has fallen! The Rim Forts are lost!"

Roland wanted to turn to them with words of encouragement, but he could think of nothing. He couldn't even bear to tell them to be quiet. At least they did not get long to wallow in their despair, because Hastafel's forces closed in from all sides and attacked.

* * * *

Sairis soon understood why he had not been able to locate the trail on the edge of the cliff. The way down started in a cave.

Sairis had been walking steeply downhill in the dark for some minutes, leading Cato by the bridle, when he found that he had enough magic for a bit of light. Sairis got back into the saddle without scrambling. His body felt strangely buoyant, as though he'd drunk a pot of strong tea.

The way was steep and narrow, but smooth enough for riding, and it was a relief to be out of the rain. He could no longer see the ghosts, although he sensed they were near.

A little further on, and he realized that he could detect the iron inside his stomach like a discreet point of irritation. He quenched it without much thought. He noticed the traces of Marsden's magic in the tin collar, too—not a real binding, but still annoying. He didn't want to deal with melted tin, so he vaporized it. *That's better.*

Sairis took a little of Cato's blood, mixed it with his own, and wrote a rune on the horse's flank. "You've got a touch of faerie somewhere in your ancestry, Cato," said Sairis to the horse. "No wonder you're such a good destrier." Sairis called out the faery blood until Cato's nostrils smoked, and his eyes glowed like red coals. The horse began to run, sure-footed in spite of the steep tunnel.

Some faint voice in Sairis's head whispered that he'd just done something impressive and perhaps alarming, but it was drowned by other thoughts that flew like birds. Sairis leafed through his textbooks in his mind's eye. He could see them as plainly as though they were in front of him. He could turn the pages and read every word. Spells that he'd only ever seen once returned with perfect clarity.

He could hear the ghosts chattering now. He told them to be quiet, and they obeyed.

Cato burst out of the tunnel all at once, and Sairis gasped in the wet, salty air. They were running down a steep switchback. Up ahead, a log half as tall as Cato lay across the trail. The horse did not slow down. Sairis watched the obstacle approach. Some part of his brain was screaming that there was a sheer drop on their right and a cliff face on their left and they needed to stop and work their way over the obstacle with care.

They did not stop. They did not slow down. Cato reached the log. He was a big, heavy horse, bred to carry knights in armor. He was not a jumper.

He jumped.

The part of Sairis's mind that was screaming seemed to lock up as they sailed over the log and landed without a stagger on the other side. Cato tossed his head and made an un-horse-like shriek.

Sairis felt the kind of thrill he'd only ever experienced in dreams. He was practically flying, and for once in his life he feared *nothing*.

The cavalry officer was suddenly beside him, almost as solid as life. "We cannot leave the mountain," he hissed.

"You can if I say so," said Sairis.

"How?"

Sairis looked calmly through the drifting mist at the carnage below. Here was the source of the magic singing in his veins. So much death, so many crossings. *I could send you into the bodies,* thought Sairis. It would be easier than trying to capture the unwilling spirits of the recently slain and force them back to fight again in life. The ghosts of Mount Cairn would enter the bodies and fight willingly. It was what Sairis would have done before…

Before his mind blossomed like a deadly flower. *The bodies are broken,* thought Sairis. *That's why they're dead. I can do better.*

Cato was flying down the switchbacks, closer and closer to the valley floor. Sairis turned his eyes away from the battlefield, westward. Clouds had boxed the valley, and the blue sparkle of the sea had turned to something darker—a sheet of reflected silver over iron waves. *Silver for binding demons,* thought Sairis. *Iron for faeries and men. I will take them all.*

Cato reached the end of a switchback, and instead of pushing him into the next turn, Sairis urged him over the embankment, not towards the middle of the valley, but towards the sea. Cato plunged downward, nimble as a mountain goat, sliding and leaping through the wet shale. He came down with hardly a stagger in sandy soil, and kept running until he splashed into the surf.

Sairis cried out. He was seeing double, seeing the River, and the thousand worlds it connected. Life and death made sense. Everything made sense. It was painful and intoxicating. It was exquisite. He could turn Cato right out of the world, ride to Faerie, ride to the astral plane, speak with demons and ghosts and the queen of the Fae. He could learn *everything.*

Something twinged in Sairis's chest—not part of himself, something *other,* something in his wards. *Roland is in trouble.*

Sairis's eyes snapped open. Cato was practically swimming. With an effort, Sairis turned him back towards shore. *I have fed you death magic, and you're as drunk on it as I am.*

Sairis sensed the ghosts of Mount Cairn—still with him, but growing rapidly weaker as they drew further from the place of their deaths. He needed to give them a vessel and soon.

Sairis took out his knife. The cut on his palm had already healed, but he did it again and trailed his hand in the sea. The waves lapped his blood as Cato splashed towards the beach.

When they stood upon the sand, Sairis slid down from the horse. He took off his shoes and stood with his feet in the sand and foam. "You have taken my blood," he said to the waves, "and now I will have a favor." Sairis thought of everything he'd read and learned in Karkaroth's tower, in books and through mirrors and even in dreams upon the Styx. He focused the magic that was burning through him like fire, and he created something new.

Sairis raised the Shattered Sea.

16

The River and the Sea

Roland did not join the men who locked shields around their position or the second and third lines behind them. He wanted to, but he knew his place at the last hour was by Daphne's side. She sat her horse at the center of their beleaguered troops, looking pale and defiant, only glancing once towards the silent bulk of Mount Cairn.

They didn't come.

Roland tried to put that thought away for later. Some part of his brain laughed. *There will be no later.*

On the battlements of the fort, Roland glimpsed a human figure, standing beside something like a bear. Except he knew it wasn't a bear. It was a wolf. *It must be satisfying to watch us die from the fort you nearly broke your teeth on.*

Anton rode towards the southern edge of the fight, calling encouragement to his troops, although his knee prevented him from actually participating. The sun shone dimly through the clouds, almost directly overhead now. The men had fought hard for hours. They were still fighting hard, but with no end in sight, their courage was wavering. Roland could practically feel the shift in morale. The salt of the sea tasted like tears.

And the golems were coming. Half a dozen of them waddled or lumbered through the rain. They'd become slathered in blood-slick mud, and several had incorporated the maimed bodies of the fallen into their torsos and limbs. Roland wondered whether that meant they had somehow entrapped the spirits of those men, or whether they simply had a ghastly instinct to collect human body parts. *Our troops will break,* thought Roland. *When those monsters reach us, they will break and run. That is when we will all die.*

Roland couldn't help glancing at the figure on the battlements. *This is when most enemy commanders would offer terms.*

"He won't," she said, her voice hollow.

Roland suspected she was right. *He gave us his terms in the conference room, and we refused. Hastafel is not the sort of person who takes rejection well.*

"It's not your fault," said Roland. "Leaders take risks. It would have worked, if..." *If our reinforcements had come.*

Daphne stared at the golems closing in. "Roland, our lines are going to break soon, and when they do, I want you to try to reach Uncle Jessup's forces in the pass. No heroics, no last stand before the gates. You ride hard for the Valley of False Hope. Perhaps it will do us one good turn at least."

Roland snorted. Escape under these circumstances was unlikely, although he supposed a few might get away. "I'll escort you in that effort."

She turned to him savagely. "No, you won't. I am not the rider you are. Not in the mountains. You are more likely to succeed on your own." She caught her breath and added in a rush, "This battle will have weakened Hastafel, and he will not be expecting a surprise attack after dark from the border lords. You can retake the fort, and if not, you may be able to starve him out by cutting him off from his ships."

Roland opened his mouth.

"You'll make a good king, Brother. If you do not wish to wed, perhaps you can point out to Uncle Winthrop that the succession will pass to his children. That may appease him."

The knot in Roland's stomach climbed into his throat. "You've...thought this through."

"Of course I have. Get ready."

"Daphne, I can't." *You're asking me to live with the knowl-edge that I left you here to die.* He stared into her steel gray eyes. *This is the way that you and Father were always tougher than me.*

"You can," she snarled. "That is an order, Roland. I suspect I will only be queen of Mistala for another ten minutes, so it's probably my last order. Please don't treat it with contempt."

Roland's vision blurred. He'd never thought to spend his last battle crying. He forced his eyes westward, still unsure what he intended to do when the lines broke. As a result, he was the first person to notice something odd at the mouth of the valley.

The rain was slackening, and the fickle wind had changed directions, blowing the clouds out to sea, improving visibility. A line of white stretched from horizon to horizon.

Roland blinked hard to clear his vision, but the line did not go away. The weather had cleared enough that he should be able to see the beach from the top of the valley. At first, Roland couldn't find it. Then he realized he was looking at a shining expanse of nearly dry sand. One of Hastafel's troop ships was sitting in mud some distance out. Roland's mouth fell open. *What in all the hells?* "Daphne..."

"I see it," she whispered. "What am I looking at?"

Roland shook his head. He caught sight of something else—a lone rider galloping from the beach. He was crossing broken, soggy ground littered with bodies and debris. He should have been picking his way with caution. Instead, he was riding all out—a small, dark figure on a big, pale horse. And behind him...

Hastafel's troop ship flipped over and disappeared. Daphne made a little noise of shock. Even at such a distance, it was a startling sight—a whole ship demolished in an instant like a toy. The line of white came on, and now Roland knew what it was. A massive wave.

The capricious sun broke from the clouds as the wind continued to blow towards the sea. It sparkled on the wall of water as it obliterated the beach and hit the mouth of the valley. Roland's eyes fixed on the rider. He'd come about halfway up the valley, but the wave behind him was coming faster.

Roland couldn't breathe. He stared at the horse. *Cato?*

There was confused shouting among Hastafel's troops. It was clear that some of them had spotted the wave, and were uncertain of what to do about it. Signal flags flashed towards the forts.

The rider was covering the ground impossibly fast, but the wave continued to catch him up. Roland felt a strange exhilaration. He had no idea what would happen next, but somehow he was glad he was alive to see it.

"Armies of Mistala," he bellowed, "hold your ground! We are not beaten! Hold! Your! Ground!"

The golems sped up. Whatever strange force animated them had clearly gotten a boost, because they moved muddy limbs faster. But the rider was upon them, and just behind him, the impossible wave. It had lost height as it came up the valley, taking on strange shapes that morphed rapidly into something familiar. Riders emerged from the water. They swung weapons that rippled and shimmered, and their horses shook manes of gleaming foam.

They fell upon Hastafel's troops, enveloping them. They washed over the golems and blasted through their muddy bodies like water through a broken damn. In seconds, the enemy lines lost all organization. Men ran shrieking, struggling out of the water, only to be dragged back down by liquid hands. Horses thrashed in the waves. Golems disintegrated, leaving behind the bones and bodies of their grisly collections.

The water ghosts did not attack the Mistalan troops or their allies, but the flood still poured in around them. "Hold!" shouted Roland. "Hold!"

Men were holding onto each other, trying to keep their footing as the rushing tide rose to the bellies of the horses. The strange rider had stopped just beyond their lines, and he sat still upon his panting beast, watching the carnage. He looked otherworldly, soaked in sea foam, his clothes in rags, streaming in the wind. His horse's eyes burned red and smoked.

Roland's horse skittered on the uncertain footing, gave a terrified neigh. Anton had backed his horse up against Daphne's. Daphne had one hand locked in the shoulder of his coat. *Is the flood going to wash us all away?*

Roland urged his horse forward, churning through the water, half-swimming. The lines parted for him, and Roland sloshed towards the dark scarecrow on the nightmare steed. Roland's own animal stopped when they were only a few paces apart and refused to go nearer.

They stared at each other as ghosts drowned Hastafel's army around them. The man's eyes behind his glasses were glowing. And they weren't black, after all. They were a very dark green.

"Sair?"

Sairis blinked.

Roland had the uncomfortable feeling that they were actually standing in a River. If he looked quickly to the right or the left, he felt certain he would see a twilit wood. His horse would disappear in a silver streak at any moment, and he and Daphne and all the rest would be caught in a current that no one could deny.

"Sair... Please." He didn't even know what he was asking for.

Sairis blinked again, as though trying to wake up. His eyes seemed to focus. "Roland."

"You came."

"I—" Sairis sat up straight in the saddle. He spoke a word that came out in a rush of black smoke and made him shudder.

The tide reversed. Suddenly it was rushing out, out, and the troops of Mistala were staggering and clinging to each other, but they were holding. Hastafel's troops didn't have a chance. Those who had not already drowned were wrapped in the embrace of watery ghosts and dragged out to sea as the wave retreated down the valley. It took bodies and equipment. It took Hastafel's camp and his war ships. It washed the valley clean, and the sun came out and sparkled on the wet earth as though nothing else had ever happened here.

Sairis began to look a bit more human as the Shattered Sea drew away. Roland noticed that he was barefoot, all of his clothes in tatters. Roland wanted to say, "What happened?" But the words that came out of his mouth were, "Your eyes are glowing."

Sairis laughed, and his face transformed in that way Roland had loved on their first meeting. Roland would have thrown his arms around him then, if his horse had been willing to approach. "I'm sorry I'm late," said Sairis. "As you have probably guessed, things went very wrong. I need to give you sad news."

Roland's eyes had fallen to the horse again. It *was* Cato, but... "First tell me what you've done to my horse!"

17

Precarious

"I can fix it," said Sairis. "It'll probably go away on its own. He's got some faery blood, and I...I..." *Gods, what did I do, exactly?* Sairis felt as though he were waking from a dream... or drifting into one. He was coming down from a great height, the way he felt sometimes when he'd been walking on the Styx and woke in his body, confused and disoriented.

Roland dismounted and approached with caution. "Well, nothing's going to threaten Cato for the moment, but he'll spook the other horses if you bring him nearer. Come on, Sair, get down, and let's go find you some clothes. I believe you've gotten my money's worth out of these."

Sairis laughed. The sound seemed to echo inside his head. *Am I full of magic or empty?* He couldn't tell. He had a burned-out sensation, as though he'd been a conduit for a great deal of power. He tried to get down from Cato, nearly fell into the mud, and Roland caught him.

Roland's armor was startlingly hard and cold, and liberally splattered with blood in every shade of wet to dry. The armor made him seem even bigger, particularly down here on the ground. The helmet made his face seem like a stranger's.

Sairis stared up at him. "You look like a knight," he whispered.

"You look like a necromancer," said Roland and kissed him.

Sairis forgot about death and battles and magic and ghosts. He did not care that Roland's gauntlets were rough against his back or that his vambrace scraped over Sairis's shoulders. Roland's armor might have been cold and alien, but his mouth was warm and achingly familiar. Sairis fetched up against the unyielding breastplate, and it didn't feel like a threat. It felt like a fortress.

Roland broke the kiss, swept Sairis off his feet, and carried him back towards the lines. Sairis's tattered clothes fluttered around them. The world rocked with every step. *I think I need a nap.*

Still, Sairis had the presence of mind to reach into the inner pocket of his coat and pull out the soggy roll of letters.

He hoped some of them were still legible. "Commander Jessup gave me these right before he died." *Well, right afterward, technically, but now's not the time to quibble.* "They're from your Uncle Winthrop to Marcus. You need to read them, Roland."

* * * *

"He was trying to get Marcus to spy for him! To control me! To...do the same thing he tried with Sairis!" Roland sat across from Daphne in the makeshift command tent that had been hastily erected from what few supplies they'd been able to scavenge in the wake of the wave.

The remains of a scant meal lay atop a tree stump, and they sat around it on chunks of driftwood that had washed up the valley. Daphne sipped weak tea from a canteen and leafed through the letters. They were all water-damaged at the edges, but the center of the roll had remained dry. Together with Sairis's recounting of the events of the previous evening, they made for damning testimony.

When Marcus refused, Uncle Winthrop sent a man to murder him...to poison him with magic. Because of me. Roland still couldn't bear to say it aloud. He felt as though he would choke on his pain and fury. "I am going to challenge him to single combat, and then I am going to kill him, Daphne. He has betrayed us in every imaginable way. Uncle Jessup was his own brother, and he—!"

"You will do nothing without my consent," she said sharply. "Roland, we are in a tricky spot. Just let me think."

Roland stood up with a growl. He had taken off his armor, but he was still wearing the sweat-soaked linen that he'd worn all day. He glanced towards Sairis, sleeping under a spare coat on one side of the tent.

"He'll be fine," said Daphne. "You should get cleaned up." Gently, she re-rolled the letters and handed them back.

Roland took the papers with an absurd sense of protectiveness. They were not only letters from Uncle Winthrop to Marcus, but also some drafts that Marcus had written and apparently never sent. The sight of his bold, messy script and familiar signature sent a pang straight through Roland's chest.

"You should get a physician to look at Anton's leg again as soon as he wakes," he told Daphne.

The Lamontian prince was asleep a few paces from Sairis, his face pale and clammy in the dim light. Roland hoped he would not lose the leg. He had pushed himself hard on a mangled knee, and the bandage was soaked with blood.

As Roland exited the tent, he saw the line of exhausted officers and advisors waiting to talk to Daphne. *She still has hard decisions to make.*

Hastafel and a small number of his inner circle remained inside the two forts. Roland did not think it could be more than a hundred men, probably less. Daphne and Lamont's troops had not yet tested Hastafel's resolve, preferring to rest and deal with their wounded. With the bulk of his army destroyed and no way to get supplies or reinforcements, Hastafel would weaken, but Roland didn't like the idea of leaving him in there for long.

What if he makes more golems or calls up monsters from the Shattered Sea?

Roland considered other possibilities as he walked through the late afternoon chill to search for clothes in the makeshift commissary. *What if he doesn't stay in the fort? What if he decides to march on down the pass into the lowlands? How much trouble could he cause with nothing but his magic and an outlaw band?*

Roland found the stream where men had been washing off the grime of battle. He stripped off and got busy with a scrub brush and a bar of soap.

To the west, the sun laid a golden track across a peaceful sea. It would set in another couple of hours. *We'll be missing our beds in the fort, then.* He had no doubt that some of the officers now speaking to Daphne were advising a full-scale assault tonight or even earlier. No one had seen any archers upon the walls, and it was even possible that Hastafel had made the decision to abandon the forts and ride into Mistala as Roland feared. However, if he decided to stay…

Without access to supplies or reinforcements, that will be a winter's siege. It will take at least that long to starve him out, and that's if we make absolutely certain that he is not relieved by sea. Zolsestrian ships will try to reach him, and they may succeed. Our current company is in no way equipped for a siege.

Hastafel might be in a tight place inside the fort, but for the moment, he was sitting on all of their food and supplies. Roland also worried about the non-combatants—squires, cooks armorers, Daphne's maids and advisors. Roland wondered whether they were barricaded inside their rooms, whether they'd managed to flee down the pass, whether they were in the stockade, whether they were dead.

At least Sairis is safe.

Several of Roland's fellow soldiers had approached him to ask cautiously after the necromancer's wellbeing. He had saved their lives, and they all knew it. *They also saw me kiss him.*

No, they didn't, Roland told himself. *I was standing with my back to the lines, and there were a thousand other things to look at.*

Another voice scoffed, *Their prince talking down a necromancer wasn't the most interesting thing on the field?*

The kiss lasted for two seconds, Roland argued. *Alright, maybe five seconds. Anyway, they didn't see!*

They did, his mind insisted. *Daphne certainly did if that long-suffering look she gave you was any indication.*

She didn't say anything, though. No one had said anything. No one ever would. They would pretend they hadn't seen, because…

Roland's thoughts were interrupted by a signal horn. *Hastafel attacking?* Roland laced up his trousers at speed and struggled up the riverbank, tucking in his shirt and trying to convince himself that he didn't feel bruised all over. He shrugged into the coat he'd found, which was too snug across the shoulders. Roland wondered with a pang whose it had been.

The signal horn was still braying the call to arms. Soldiers who'd been asleep on the ground with their heads on their packs were jumping to their feet, blearily searching for weapons. Roland came out of the trees, straining his eyes towards the fort.

But the gates had not opened. Nothing had changed.

With a sense of mounting unease, Roland glanced towards Mount Cairn.

In the distance, the setting sun reflected off the armor of long, orderly lines of troops, switchbacking out of the clouds. *The border lords.*

This should have been good news. Here were reinforcements with food, fresh weapons, clothing, tents, and other supplies. Here were fresh men and horses to overwhelm Hastafel's scant troops in the forts or begin a proper siege. This should have been salvation.

Roland thought of Sairis, of Uncle Jessup, and he was not reassured. He looked towards Daphne's patchwork command tent, at their exhausted men struggling back into battered armor. He thought of their empty bellies. *This could get ugly.*

18

Nothing Else for Later

It took forty minutes for the vanguard of the border lords to reach the bottom of the valley and cross the open ground to Daphne's encampment. Forty minutes for tired, hungry men to dress, arm, and organize themselves. Forty minutes for Daphne to brief her officers and advisors on their situation. Forty minutes for Roland to wake Sairis, explain to him what was happening, and get him dressed in dry clothes and onto a horse. After some debate, Roland decided to continue riding the horse he'd acquired and let Sairis stay on Cato. The destrier's eyes were no longer red or smoking, but his teeth seemed a bit too sharp when he curled his lip. *If Sairis has to run, I want him on this horse.*

Daphne rode up beside them as Sairis was climbing into the saddle. "I don't think that's a good idea, Roland."

"I'm not leaving him here," said Roland.

"I could possibly be helpful," offered Sairis. Roland could tell that he was having trouble waking up, but he held out his palm and flame blossomed, burning green around the edges.

"That will not be helpful," said Daphne bluntly. "These are our own people, our reinforcements for gods' sakes!"

"They abandoned us to die," said Roland.

"Uncle Winthrop, perhaps," said Daphne, "but I'm not willing to declare civil war just yet. I do not want them to feel threatened."

"That should be easy as long as they don't threaten us," said Roland.

Daphne shook her head. "The Crown *cannot* be at war with the border lords, Roland. It would cause unimaginable chaos. This is not a fight that can be won with swords or fireballs or walking corpses."

Roland opened his mouth to say something angry, something like, *They crossed that line when they murdered Uncle Jessup.*

But Sairis spoke first, "Understood, Your Grace. And I will stay here if you think that will make it easier. I take it Anton is not coming?"

"Anton is feverish and cannot sit a horse," said Daphne, and Roland felt sorry for his anger.

"That always happens after such a wound," said Roland. "He's strong. He'll pull through."

Daphne shut her eyes, and Roland was reminded of his own way of handling pain. *She's putting that away for later.* She opened her eyes and nodded. "Sairis can come with us. But no threats."

"Understood."

Roland thought, however, that her actions belied her words. Daphne roused what remained of her army, and they marched at her back in full array when she met her uncle on the field moments later. She might not want a fight, but she was prepared for one. Unfortunately, Roland feared it would be brief. As the strength of the border lords continued to flow down out of the pass, he wondered whether even fireballs would stop them. He also felt a sick sense of helpless frustration. *Where were all of you when my men were dying here this morning?*

Their pristine armor and clean weapons seemed like a taunt to the battered, bloodied remains of the army that stood behind Daphne.

Winthrop Malconwy rode with a dozen of the most powerful lords at the head of the column, their banners snapping in the wind, the evening light catching on their armor. Roland wondered what Winthrop must be thinking as he spied his niece and nephew still alive. *That wasn't your plan, was it, Uncle?*

However, by the time he reached them, his face was stern and expressionless behind his beard. The men around him looked equally unfriendly. Daphne and Winthrop's horses stopped a few paces from one another, and their people fanned out to either side.

The wave had left vast swathes of standing water in the already-boggy ground of the valley. Their horses were wading through mud and shallow pools. The tramp of feet continued down the mountain behind them. *Splash, splash, splash…*

There was a long, uncertain pause. No one hailed the queen. No one thanked the gods for her victory. No one offered apologies or explanations for their tardy arrival. No one said anything.

At last, Daphne cleared her throat. "Uncle, you are late."

Winthrop inclined his head. "I am, Niece."

Roland could not help himself, *"Your Grace,"* he corrected, his voice tight with fury.

Winthrop shot him an unreadable look and then continued to Daphne. "I am late because the necromancer Sairis escaped his bonds yet again, aided by the traitor, Marsden. They set a fort on fire and murdered my brother."

"I have heard Sairis's version of this story," said Daphne. "I believe you are mistaken. Sairis provided us with aid, without which I and my people would all be dead."

One of the border lords spoke. "We have concerns, Your Grace, about battles won with necromancy."

"Would you prefer that I had died, my lord?"

"Of course not, Your Grace. We would prefer that Commander Jessup had not died, either."

The barons were murmuring to each other and shooting glances at Sairis. Roland caught the words "poisoned victory cup" and "viper in our bosom."

Winthrop's gaze settled on Daphne. "There is a concern among the lords, Your Grace, that the necromancer Sairis has gained undue influence over you," he paused a long beat and added, "and especially over Roland."

Roland could sense Daphne's sudden tension. He felt a sick sense of helplessness.

Winthrop continued in a low voice that did not carry to those farther out. "As I've said before, certain irregularities in Roland's habits have been noted by witnesses. I do not think we need to go into detail at this time. Please understand that I wish to preserve our family's dignity." He smiled and it was a nasty expression that did not touch his eyes.

Daphne spoke through gritted teeth. "What are you proposing, Uncle?"

"You will declare me regent," said Winthrop, "until such time as we can be certain that you are not under the influence of magic. The lords and I have already spoken of this and agreed that it would be a good temporary measure that would satisfy them."

Roland snorted. *As though Daphne would ever see the throne again.*

"A counteroffer," said Daphne, "I will abdicate to Roland."

Everyone went still. Roland could hardly believe what he was hearing. *No.* "Daphne..." But she shot him such a ferocious expression that he shut his mouth.

Winthrop seemed just as startled. "I do not believe this settles the question of the necromancer's influence—"

"You would prefer a male heir," interrupted Daphne. "There has been too much change too fast in our kingdom. Very well. You will accept my marriage to Anton Lamont, binding us as allies, but not uniting our two countries in future generations. Roland will rule Mistala. Furthermore, if Roland chooses not to wed, the succession will pass to your children, Uncle."

That got Winthrop's attention. Roland saw the unmistakable hungry gleam. He wanted to scream. *You should be on trial for murder. Instead, you're being given a chance to shape the next ruler.*

Daphne… You've trained your whole life to sit a throne, to govern. You enjoy it. You're good at it! You are giving up your dreams and your future. To protect me from shame."

He could almost hear Daphne saying, *"We are outnumbered, Roland, and our men are hungry and exhausted. The border lords could crush us. I am doing what must be done."*

Think about it later, he told himself. *Do what you have to do, and think about it later.*

No.

Roland began to laugh. Everyone stared at him, but he kept laughing. Then he was weeping, tears running into his beard. Sairis ventured to put a hand on his shoulder. His voice came out in an uncertain whisper. "Roland?"

But Roland just shook his head. He didn't know how to say, *I didn't cry when my friends died. I only shed a handful of tears for Marcus. I didn't cry when I got the news about Father. Or when I learned that at least one of my uncles doesn't love me. My sister is about to pay a terrible price to keep a secret that everyone already knows. And I can't save anything else for later.*

"You see," began Winthrop to the men around him, "this is the instability I spoke of—"

"Men of Mistala!" bellowed Roland in his best battlefield voice. "My uncle is attempting to manipulate my sister the queen with a family secret!"

"Roland…" began Daphne.

At the same time, Winthrop growled, "Have a care, Nephew. If you wish to reign—"

"I don't," said Roland and then shouted, "I am an invert!"

The troops went so quiet that Roland could hear the distant sound of the surf. *Alistair was right,* he thought sadly. *Poor fool. My own citizen, and I failed him. He wanted to make me different so that I would understand. He didn't know that I was already different…that people like me can hide in plain sight. But the secret still comes at too high a price.*

"I have preferred men since I became old enough to think of such things," continued Roland loudly. "I was in love with Marcus Kinnic—an excellent soldier as you all know. I wished to have a committed relationship with him as most men wish with their beloved, but he was taken from me in battle. I learned recently that my own uncle, Lord Winthrop, had him poisoned because he would not agree to spy upon me. Commander Jessup had proof of this. Lord Winthrop murdered him for it and tried to blame this on Magus Sairis."

Now the talking broke out. It buzzed like angry bees through the ranks, a ripple that ran out and out from those who were close enough to hear Roland's words to those who hadn't caught everything.

Winthrop had turned an unpleasant shade of puce. "Roland, you have brought shame on our family!"

"No, that would be you, sir," said Daphne. She was smiling at Roland, her expression amazed and a little uncertain, almost fragile. Roland had never seen that look from Daphne before.

In a softer voice, Roland said to her, "I thought I was protecting you by keeping this secret, Daphne. But I wasn't. I was protecting myself. I've been letting *you* protect me for far too long. I've given other people a weapon they could use to hurt us. No more."

He turned to Sairis, who was watching wide-eyed. "It has been a year since I lost Marcus," continued Roland to the troops. "I did not think I would find love again, but I have. Magus Sairis has endured extensive persecution from my family, and yet he risked his life to save Daphne and me when Hastafel attacked us in the palace. He has been a kind and trustworthy friend in spite of all the abuse that has been hurled at him in my presence. He has repeatedly gotten between me and deadly magic, and he recently turned the tide of a battle that was lost when our reinforcements did not appear. I love him and will continue to do so, and I will challenge any man who impugns his honor."

Sairis actually blushed. By the end of the speech, he'd fixed his eyes somewhere in the vicinity of Cato's ears.

The lords were muttering furiously. Winthrop kept interjecting things like, "You can't possibly believe any of this," and, "They are under a spell!"

Roland backed up a little to lay a hand on Sairis's shoulder. "Sorry to embarrass you," he murmured, "but it had to be said."

Sairis swallowed, nodded, patted his hand.

Roland raised his head high and gazed out over the men. A few looked back. Most looked quickly away. He saw carefully neutral expressions punctuated by flashes of curiosity, shock, or disgust. He also caught a few knowing smiles and even a few looks of frank admiration.

Some of these people will tell their own truths this evening because I was brave, Roland realized. *I was the only one who could do this. Because Daphne is right. I am untouchable. I am the premier knight of the realm. No one can hurt me with this secret unless I give it power. I can make the world safer for people like me, like Sairis, like Marsden, like November and Hazel. Perhaps even like Alistair. But only if I am willing to suffer a little embarrassment, some disrespect from fools, a bit of disgust from old men.* It didn't hurt nearly as much as he'd expected.

One of the lords turned from the huddle to glare at Daphne. "Is there any proof of these accusations against Lord Winthrop, Your Grace?"

"There are letters in his own hand to Marcus Kinnic."

"I have them right here," said Roland.

"And I think," continued Daphne, "that if you will listen calmly to Sairis's version of events in the fort, you'll find it enlightening."

"He's a necromancer!" howled Winthrop. "He has seduced my nephew into unspeakable depravity!"

"Yes, we've established that," snapped one of the lords. "However, I believe this situation is best settled by a trial before a jury, where we can see all the evidence and decide for ourselves." He turned to Daphne. "Your Grace, I hope you realize that we were under certain assumptions when we arrived here today..."

Daphne gave them all a tight smile. "I will consider this a misunderstanding, my lords, as long as my men can promptly receive food, shelter, and medical care. I'd also like to know what happened to Magus Marsden, who is certainly not a traitor."

"He has not been seen since the fire, My Queen, though there was an attempt to take him prisoner."

Lord Winthrop was staring around with a baffled expression, as though he couldn't quite understand what was happening. Roland kicked his own horse forward, reached his uncle and said, "You will surrender your sword, sir. You will be under guard until your trial. Count yourself lucky if we do not chain you like a common murderer."

Winthrop seemed to swell like an angry toad. "How *dare* you?" He reached for the hilt of his weapon, and Roland drew his own blade in one smooth movement.

"Daphne has forbidden me to challenge you to single combat," he snarled. "But please do give me an excuse."

Winthrop was breathing hard now, his eyes flicking around the group. Roland thought he would say something else, but he seemed to think better of it and subsided. He did not resist when one of the men beside him unbuckled Winthrop's sword belt and tossed the weapon to Roland.

They were interrupted by the desperate blaring of a signal horn. The note was so high and so strident that Roland felt certain the sentry had missed something and was trying to make up for lost time. *I suppose I did have everyone distracted…*

He turned, half expecting to see troops pouring out of the Rim Forts, perhaps with sorcerous reinforcements. Instead, he saw a lone man. He carried a white flag, and an enormous black wolf loped beside him.

19

Vengeance

Sairis had to give credit where it was due—Hastafel did not lack for courage. He was alone except for his demon, facing thousands of men who would love to see him shredded. And yet he moved with no sign of nerves. *Of course,* thought Sairis, *he put all his fear and self-doubt in the sword, so perhaps that's not so impressive after all.*

The sorcerer had already skirted the carnage before the gates of the southern fort. He stopped when he found a clear spot amid a vast swath of standing water, like a shallow lake.

He rammed his white flag into the mud, bade his wolf lie down at his feet, crossed his arms, and waited.

All along the lines, bowstrings went taut, but the white flag made them hesitate.

Daphne was craning her neck, standing in her stirrups. "Sairis, what is he doing?"

"I don't know, but I doubt he's surrendering."

"Should we shoot him?"

Sairis shrugged. "I doubt arrows will harm him, and he might retaliate."

"Should I challenge him?" asked Roland.

"No," said Sairis and Daphne at the same time.

Daphne scowled in concentration. Then she snapped out orders for troops to circle around behind Hastafel, cutting him off from the fort.

"Is it safe to talk to him, Sairis?"

"No. But it might be the only way to end this."

Daphne nodded. She turned to the barons and said, "Well, my lords, it appears that you are not too late to share in the glory of our victory. Although using an entire army to crush a single sorcerer may be overkill. Let's go finish this."

Sairis didn't think the barons looked excited about their opportunity for glory. However, there wasn't much they could say, and orders flew for the troops to march after the queen as they all converged on the figure of Hastafel, who looked as though he were standing on a sheet of still water. It reflected the golden light of sunset like a mirror.

Roland had taken charge of Winthrop in the absence of anyone else to do the job. The duke's initial outrage had subsided, and he was affecting a haughty air of disinterest. Sairis was sure he was planning his legal defense and what favors he might be able to call from his many friends and contacts.

As they drew closer to the solitary figure, Sairis got a better look at Hastafel. He was dressed in furs and leather. No sign of a weapon.

Daphne and her entourage stopped about twenty feet away, and troops fanned out to either side, forming a rapidly closing circle. Hastafel watched without apparent concern. He'd clearly fought in the battle today. His leather armor showed scars of recent use. His black hair was streaked with silver that he'd made no effort to magic away, and it ruffled in the sea wind. Even standing there alone, he looked like a leader, a hero even. Sairis understood why mountain tribes and abused peasants had followed him, why they'd believed that he would save them and unite the Shattered Sea under one ruler. *Perhaps you really were a hero a decade ago. You just never knew when to stop fighting.*

The wolf stood up, its red eyes flicking around Daphne's retinue. It did not growl or bristle. It just stood there, waiting.

Sairis was a little disconcerted when the warlord looked directly at him and smiled. "Ah, the apprentice." His voice was a low rasp—the voice of a man who has been shouting for hours. "For a moment this morning, I thought they'd let Karkaroth out of his tower. I seem to have underestimated you rather spectacularly, Magus…Sairis, isn't it?"

Sairis's mouth ran away with his brain as Cato came to a stop. "Well, I was the best they could do."

Hastafel gave a dry laugh.

He turned to Daphne. "When we last spoke, Your Grace, I told you that the kingdoms of the Shattered Sea will be ruled by magic. You seem to have chosen necromancy over sorcery."

Out of the corner of his eye, Sairis saw the lords shifting in their saddles, glancing at each other.

"I believe that the kingdoms of the Shattered Sea will need to take counsel from magicians," said Daphne. "I do not believe we need become fiefdoms. Sairis has never attacked me or waged war on my people. Now let's talk about why you're out here. I trust you wish to discuss the terms of your surrender?"

Hastafel gave her an appraising look. "I think you'll agree we are at an impasse, Queen. I am in a position to give you trouble for a long time. My men can hold the Rim Forts through an extensive siege, as you well know. We can reach your kingdom before you have time to go around the forts through the mountains. In fact, I think it likely that I might reach your capital before you do."

Sairis felt a chill.

"You can't do that without leaving the forts unguarded," said Daphne. "Your army is broken, Hastafel. You can continue your assault on my kingdom with a handful of people, but I promise in the end I will crush you. Meanwhile, rumors will run north and south that the great sorcerer's armies are no more. Governments you have left in your wake will topple. If you meant what you said about magic ruling the Shattered Sea, you would be best advised to look to your existing conquests. Go home, and *rule.*"

These were level-headed words, although Sairis could see that the border lords didn't like them.

"If we let him walk out of here alive, we'll never see the end of this," muttered someone.

"Soft on magic," growled another.

Sairis glanced at the wolf. *Is it exerting itself?* He wished he knew more about demons.

The sorcerer inclined his head. "Valid points, Your Grace. Although, I do think you underestimate the trouble I am capable of causing."

Sairis doubted that. He just thought Daphne had a good political face.

"Here are my terms," said Hastafel. "You will allow me and my remaining followers to depart along the coast. There will be no further hostilities between us, nor will I harm your people who are still alive in the fort." He hesitated a moment, his eyes flicking around at them. "In exchange, you will return my sword, which I rather thoughtlessly left in your necromancer."

Daphne frowned. "The sword…?"

"We don't have it," said Sairis and Roland at the same time.

Hastafel's expression did not change. "I believe you do."

Sairis heard the barons muttering again.

"I require the sword to properly manage my creature," said Hastafel, his eyes flicking briefly to the wolf. "I think you'll agree that it would be irresponsible of me to neglect such a thing."

"We don't have the sword," said Daphne.

The wolf spoke. "You do." Its voice was more cultured than Sairis had expected. Its red eyes drifted over the company and Sairis felt...something.

This was a mistake. "Stop!" he snapped out. "Whatever you're doing, stop right now unless you want another dose of necromantic fire!"

"I am not doing anything," purred the wolf.

Somewhere behind him, Sairis heard a sword drawn. "Necromancy was always the scourge of Mistala. Damned if we're going to start celebrating it now!"

"Inverts in line for the throne. This cannot be borne."

"The weakness of women will be the death of us."

Daphne looked at Sairis in confusion. "What is happening?"

"It is Wrath," said Sairis. "It can't create rage, only draw it out. However, I'm afraid it has plenty to work with here."

Daphne turned to say something to the men behind her... and one of the guards with the border lords leapt off his horse. His clothes melted and ran together into black smoke as he moved.

The wolf's smug expression changed. "You!" it snarled as Mal rematerialized as a leopard.

Hastafel's composure slipped for the first time. "Malcharius! Why are you still here? I have dismissed you!"

"Several times," agreed Mal as he circled the wolf. "But, you see, you didn't summon me. Not exactly."

Another guard jumped down from his horse. He looked like an ordinary soldier, but the voice that emerged was Candice's. "Phillip Gosling of the murdered village of Hastafel, I bind you to my will." She followed this with a spell that cracked through the moist air.

Her words had an astonishing effect. Lord Hastafel crumpled as though he'd been shot. His knees hit the soggy ground with a splash, and he doubled over. *She's trying to bind him!* realized Sairis. *The first iteration of Hastafel's ghost... He must have given her his name!*

"Fernus!" shrieked Hastafel in a voice that was hardly recognizable. "Kill her!"

No one needed to be told who Fernus was. The wolf jerked towards Candice like a dog on a leash, but Mal barreled into him, and the two of them flipped over in a splashing blur of bloody foam.

Candice's glamour fell away as she ran towards Hastafel, who was struggling to stand, his face a rictus of shock and pain. "Dismiss that wolf!" she shouted. "I command you!"

Hastafel responded with a flash of blue flame, but he was clearly having difficulty, and he missed her by several feet. *The demon is the source of his magic,* thought Sairis. *She'll have a hard time binding Hastafel as long as he's got an astral entity to draw from.* Sairis could sense the demon Wrath, its magic strong in the air as it struggled with Mal's Lust magic. The combination was disconcerting. All around him, men were backing away or drawing weapons, looking for something to fight, or possibly something to fuck. *These two armies were on the verge of attacking each other minutes ago. All they need is one careless arrow.*

"Marsden!" shouted Sairis. *You've got to be here. I'd bet any amount of magic you put that glamour on Candice.* "Where *is* the sword?" *If we could put the wolf back inside it, Candice's spell might work.*

"I don't know!" The guard who'd been riding beside Candice was suddenly familiar. "It was taken during the fire! I was hoping someone would—"

A soft grunt. Sairis couldn't have said how he caught it over the snarls of the two fighting demons, but it seemed to bypass his ears and go straight to his chest. He turned to see Roland still sitting his horse very close to Winthrop Malconwy. Roland had a startled expression on his face, one hand clenched around his left shoulder at the join of the armor.

Winthrop was holding a familiar glossy blade, crawling with runes and now slick with blood. He must have been keeping it in whatever spelled sheath or distortion field Marsden had used to conceal it. His eyes glittered with hate, all sense of restraint or self-preservation obliterated by the spirit of Wrath. "I will not have my family honor impugned by *you!*" he spat at Roland. "You have shamed our name before our own barons! You are no nephew of mine! No doubt your mother was a whore who got you from some perverse act with a witch!"

As Roland swayed in the saddle, Winthrop reached inside his nephew's coat and jerked out the roll of Marcus's letters. He folded them over the sword once, twice, thrice, and sliced again and again. The fragments of soggy paper fluttered into the muddy water beneath their horses' hooves.

"The fact that you buggered your father's ward proves nothing except that you are a pervert! The fact that I disapproved and tried to conceal your shame proves only that I am an honorable man!" snarled Winthrop into Roland's increasingly pale face.

One of the lords near Winthrop made a grab for his reins, but Winthrop set the blade beside Roland's throat and shouted. "Do not dare to lay hands upon me! I am taking my pretender of a nephew and returning to my lands. Those of you who do not wish to be ruled by women and inverts may join me! Daphne, if you so much as send a scout after me, I will cut this creature's throat!"

Sairis looked towards the demons. Mal had backed off, panting and bleeding. The wolf was standing in front of Hastafel's slumped body, its eyes very bright. It was feeding on Winthrop's rage, Sairis was certain.

Sairis turned back towards Roland. Blood was now visibly seeping around his armpit. Some of the shock had left his face, replaced by bewildered anger. He was going to make a grab for the sword. When he did, Winthrop would kill him… if he hadn't already. Sairis thought of the ghosts endlessly flinging themselves around the moat of a tower in the mist, their voices weeping. Untenable solutions flicked fruitlessly through his head. *Think!*

Sairis's eyes fell to the water, to the fragments of letters, floating in all that remained of his wave. A drop of Roland's blood hit the ripples and curled down among the torn pages. Roland's blood…still laced with necromantic magic. And papers signed by a murdered man with his true name.

Oh.

A hand broke the surface. Winthrop's horse shied, forcing him back from Roland as a liquid shape reared out of the muddy water. Bits of paper floated through its body. *"Vengeance,"* thought Sairis and almost laughed. It was the cavalry officer who had led him down Mount Cairn.

"Marcus?" whispered Roland.

Winthrop stared at the ghost, his eyes bulging from his face. He gave a wordless cry and slashed through its neck with Hastafel's sword. The blood on the blade curled through the water. Rather than disintegrating, the ghost gained definition. His hair took on a touch of red. "Murderer," he hissed.

"No!" shrieked Winthrop. "This is black magic, dark sorcery! Don't you all see? This is deception! Perversion!"

"You murdered me," rasped the spirit.

"Marcus?" repeated Roland, reaching for the ghost in spite of his obvious pain and fear.

The ghost raised its eyes to him. Sairis was impressed that it could muster attention for more than its primary objective. Spirits that lingered did not often retain complex interests or desires. They tended to become quite single-minded. However, the ghost looked at Roland for long enough that Winthrop took the opportunity to stab it again.

The spirit made an animal shriek. It turned to Winthrop, opened its arms wide, and poured itself into him.

No Regrets

Winthrop Malconwy drowned. He drowned while sitting upright in his saddle, flailing, voiceless as water poured into his nose and throat. Roland thought, at the end, that he ought to feel some trace of sorrow or regret. But he felt nothing. He thought that he should say something to Marcus.

Could Marcus even hear him? Could anyone?

The world seemed wrapped in linen gauze. Through a fog, he saw Candice running towards the fallen sword, but Hastafel's demon reached it first. The wolf's form vanished into red smoke, and he scooped up the sword as a towering knight in red armor.

"Kill her!" repeated Hastafel.

Roland missed what happened next. He was on the ground somehow, and Sairis was leaning over him. Men were shouting. Horses' hooves tramped dangerously around their heads. Roland couldn't seem to sit up. Sairis was fumbling at the ties and clasps of his breastplate, cursing. His skin crawled with lines of green light.

Roland managed to speak. "Did he get me…that badly?"

"It's the sword," panted Sairis. "It traps ghosts; that's what it does."

"I feel…strange."

Sairis had exposed the wound in his armpit. Roland didn't think it was mortal. His chest should not feel so heavy.

Sairis leaned over him, his eyes intent behind his glasses. He smiled through an expression that looked like pain. "Resonance. It works both ways." He caught his breath and added, "I regret nothing. Remember that. Not one thing, Roland."

Then Sairis slumped forward, and Roland could breathe again.

* * * *

Sairis sat on the banks of the River. *No. Not the River. The moat.*

His ghostly senses insisted that it was the River, that he should jump in, shed this useless form, and fly downstream. *He'd felt the call before, but it was so much stronger now that he was...dead?*

This is a trap.

Sairis raised his eyes with an effort. The tower rose above him. It looked bigger, somehow, and darker. He could feel his connection to it like a chain. He was bound, tethered. He would never escape its pull. He would spin in circles forever, feeding the magic that had built this place. He would forget Karkaroth, his goals, his studies. He would even forget Roland and the reason he'd flung himself into this trap. In time, he would forget everything that made him unique, but he would not be gone. Not quite. And the unquenchable longing for oblivion would never end.

The weight of that knowledge was almost unbearable. *The sooner I forget, the better.*

Sairis slipped into the water.

And came up short with a jerk.

"Simon Harris, come back..." He felt the words, but he didn't really understand them. Something had him. He thrashed like a fish on a line as he was drawn inexorably back to the base of the tower. A person stood there. Sairis's spirit senses interpreted him as a ghost, but some shred of wizardly intuition remained, and he identified the aura as a glamour.

"Simon Harris, come back," repeated the other, and Sairis remembered his own form like a discarded glove, still familiar. He put it back on.

"Andrew?"

Sairis thought that he ought to feel intimidated, given the circumstances. But Marsden was staring around, wide-eyed. He looked lost.

"You don't spirit-walk," whispered Sairis.

Marsden's face and form flickered as though he were composed of overlapping images. Sairis could see traces of the girl he'd once been, but more than that, he could see his true age. Marsden was nearly contemporary with his master, a fact that Sairis easily forgot. His spirit was tattered—many versions of himself, stitched together by his long and complicated life.

Sairis thought about Karkaroth's attempts to bring his former lover into the Shadow Lands. *But Andrew never came here...until now.*

"Who told you?" asked Sairis.

Marsden seemed to pull himself together. "Your name? Roland. I could get it out of your glasses, but there isn't time. I've bound you to your body..."

Sairis gave a sad smile. "That doesn't work for long."

"I know. But you're not mortally wounded, Sairis. Your ghost is just trapped."

"You came to the Shadow Lands to bring me back?"

Marsden didn't answer. He was staring at the dark and twisted trees beyond the moat, at the beguiling twilight of the wood.

"It's beautiful, isn't it?" whispered Sairis.

"No. Yes." Marsden shook his head. "Sairis, how do we break this thing? The wolf was locked in here to guard it. The wolf is gone. We should be able to destroy it."

Sairis cocked an eyebrow at him. "You think I wouldn't have already done that if I knew how? It's older than the Sundering, Andrew." He took a deep breath. "And I'm just an apprentice who should have stayed in his tower."

"You were more than ready to leave that tower. And there are two of us now."

Sairis laughed. "A sheltered university magician and a baby necromancer."

Marsden rolled his eyes. "A cautious professor and a reckless prodigy."

You think I'm a prodigy? Sairis didn't know how to respond, so he gestured quickly towards the drawbridge, just visible in the low-hanging mist. "I tried to cross last time, but there were still wards. Strong ones. I'm not sure how they're being maintained. If you walk around the tower, you can see the place where the original creator channeled the Styx into the moat. There's probably a way to reverse it, but I don't think I have time."

"Show me," said Marsden.

As before, no monsters threatened them at the drawbridge, but a sign flickered into existence on the far side: "None but my master shall pass."

Marsden stared at it for a long moment. "This is recent," he said at last. "You say there are wards?"

Sairis nodded. "It's what's kept the hungry ghosts from wandering. I don't understand how the wards are being renewed."

Marsden advanced to the edge of the bridge, examining the ground carefully. "Offhand, I'd say it's because some*one* is renewing them." There was an edge to his voice that Sairis couldn't interpret. "Let's see this dry ditch."

They walked around the outside of the moat, sticking close to the edge so as not to trigger the wards. The ghosts flashed past in the water, their keening loud in the still air. Twice, green flames jumped up somewhere in the distance, warning a ghost off from the perimeter.

When they reached the dry ditch, Sairis was not surprised to see one of the ghosts sitting on the edge, staring towards the Styx. As he got closer, however, he noticed inconsistencies. The aura wasn't quite right. The details of the figure were a little too well-defined. *This is a spirit-walker. Another magician. Who...?*

And then he knew.

Sairis felt dizzy as he covered the remaining distance and sat down on the edge of the ditch. He could sense Marsden somewhere behind him, hesitating.

The spirit sitting beside Sairis looked like a wizened little man with bird-bright eyes and an unkempt beard, which was long enough for him to twist absently around one finger. A bony hand clasped a knobby knee through the fabric of worn work trousers. His eyes remained on the distant gleam of the Styx.

Sairis cleared his throat. "Sir?"

The necromancer Karkaroth turned and looked at his apprentice. They stared at each other for a long moment. Then Karkaroth said severely, "How long have you been gone and who is cleaning the pigeon boxes?"

Sairis couldn't help himself. Even as a spirit, his eyes flooded. "You have been asleep for the better part of a year, sir. Your pulse is so soft and so slow that I can hardly feel it. Your breath is undetectable. Your body is…is shutting down, sir."

Karkaroth had never seemed to know how to respond to displays of emotion. He looked at Sairis in bewilderment. At last he said, "Is it, then? Well. A year, you say? Losing my body… That could be inconvenient."

"Inconvenient!" howled Sairis. "I have been alone, trying to figure out how to…how to help you and what to do if you're gone, and I am so…" *I was so alone.*

Karkaroth hesitated. His posture deflated a little. At last, he said, "I would have thought you'd have run away to that university by now."

Sairis wiped his face on his sleeve. *Damned body, still remembering to be human.* "I thought if I figured out how to restore the wood, you might be alright. I…I left the tower. I thought I was only going to be gone for a few days, but it's been weeks. I was stabbed and kidnapped and poisoned. I raised elk and humans and even the Shattered Sea. I rode a horse and I made friends and I fell in love. And all I wanted to do was save you!"

Karkaroth smiled. He looked a little more alive now, a little more human. He studied his apprentice. "Fell in love, eh? With whom?"

Sairis sniffled. "You'd *kill* me."

Karkaroth waved a hand. "Love is a mannerless houseguest. It stalks in uninvited and leaves footprints all over the rugs. Love never arrives at a time that would be rational or convenient."

Sairis hiccupped a laugh. "He's a knight."

Karkaroth shrugged. "I once fell in love with a nobleman's daughter. Can you imagine? Me! One step away from aristocracy!" He gave an exaggerated shudder.

Sairis barked a laugh.

"But it was good for a while," continued his teacher. "I've often thought those were my happiest years."

Someone spoke behind them. "Were they?"

Karkaroth glanced over his shoulder. A long pause and then he said softly, "Ari?"

Marsden came forward and sat down on the other side of him—not too close. Karkaroth cocked his head. "Have you come to put me down at last? Gods, you must want it badly to cross over."

Marsden shook his head. "I came for Sairis. To get him out of here before his body dies." Marsden hesitated. "Have you been keeping these ghosts contained all this time?"

Karkaroth nodded. "I found the tower a few years ago when some villagers asked me to deal with a malevolent spirit. It had wandered onto the mortal plane. I tracked it back to this place."

A bitter smile flickered around the corners of Marsden's mouth. "Protecting Mistala in your own way?"

Karkaroth harrumphed. "You always wanted to think so. It always got you into trouble."

"Figuring out how to build your own?" asked Marsden dryly.

Karkaroth shrugged. "It's very interesting."

"We need to destroy it," said Marsden, "if you want Sairis to survive."

"You're always after my towers," grumbled Karkaroth.

Marsden passed a hand over his face. "I wish you had come down."

Sairis was surprised when Karkaroth said, "So do I." There was a long silence. At last, he continued, "I...lost my temper, Ari."

"I noticed," muttered Marsden. "The whole kingdom noticed."

Karkaroth jerked a gnarled thumb at Sairis. "But that kid... taking him in was the best thing I ever did."

Sairis was shocked. His master had never said such a thing before. Indeed, he'd commented on many occasions at the massive inconvenience that Sairis presented.

"The world isn't kind to people like him," continued Karkaroth. "I hoped he'd be like me—content with his magic and his books—but he's not. He's lonely."

"He has made friends," said Marsden quietly. "He has proven himself talented, kind, and loyal. He has superb control of his own magic. My school would be a better place with him in it."

Karkaroth's eyes narrowed suspiciously. "You'll put a collar on him?"

"No," whispered Marsden. He took a deep breath. "I made mistakes, too, Jonas. We need people like Sairis. I was hoping he could help me with some of the others."

"Or *you* could!" interjected Sairis to Karkaroth. "Sir, you know so much, and you're not a very patient teacher, but you taught me, and—"

Karkaroth was laughing. "I am not a professor, Sair." His sharp little eyes gleamed. "I am a dark wizard, who has followed knowledge into inexcusable places."

"But—"

He stood up and stretched. "I have actually been thinking about how to unravel this spirit vessel. The ghosts could break the wall of the moat if they all struck together. They would need an incentive to do that, however. A powerful one. They would need someone to lead the way."

Sairis understood an instant before Marsden. He got to his feet. "No."

"Sair, I am old. As you said, my body is failing."

"No."

He touched Sairis's cheek—a parental gesture that seemed utterly alien to Sairis. "*You* are the only thing that was keeping me on the mortal plane, child. And as you've just pointed out, I was doing a terrible job at that, too. You don't need me anymore."

Tears ran down Sairis's face.

Karkaroth stepped away. "When I cut the tether to my body, a great deal of necromantic magic will be released. The ghosts will come like sharks to blood. They'll follow me down the ditch into the true River...into Death."

Marsden cleared his throat. "What about the fragments of Hastafel's ghost? Will they also...die?"

Karkaroth considered. "Gods, I wish I was going to get to see that part! I'm not sure what they'll do, but I suspect they'll rejoin their host like a demon returning to its entity." His eyes crinkled. "Maybe Sair can come back and tell me what happened."

Marsden frowned. "You're planning to linger?"

Karkaroth laughed—more of a cackle, really. "I'm a necromancer. Everyone knows we're bad at dying."

Marsden massaged the bridge of his nose. "Jonas, please don't make me hunt you down. Again."

Karkaroth shrugged. "I admit, I'm curious about what's beyond the gate. So maybe I won't linger after all."

Sairis threw his arms around the old man, who accepted this familiarity with all the grace of a feral cat. He disengaged and turned away with a wave of his hand. "Bury me under my favorite tree. You know the place, but never tell another soul. And burn that book we got from the faery prince; it's nothing but trouble. Do *not* let Ari burn the rest of my library!"

"I will," said Sairis. "And I won't!"

"Make sure the pigeons are cared for, and water the beans."

"Yes, sir."

Then he dropped into the ditch in a flash of green flame and all hell broke loose inside the moat.

21

Hastafel

Sairis jerked awake. A big man was looming over him with a drawn sword in the waning light. For a moment, he was eleven years old and standing in a bean patch, staring up at a knight. Then his head cleared. "Roland?"

Roland's gaze was focused outwards, but he looked down quickly. "Sair?"

Sairis registered Marsden sitting up beside him. "How long?" gasped the old man. "How long were we gone?"

"A couple of minutes?" said Roland, his voice full of distracted relief. "Sair, don't you ever do that again!"

"Can't promise," whispered Sairis, adjusting his glasses.

"I couldn't live with myself!"

"You took Marsden's spell for me. It was my turn." Sairis wanted to make a better joke, but he just couldn't summon one. *My teacher is gone.*

"What's happening with Hastafel?" asked Marsden

"Not sure," said Roland. "Daphne ordered everyone back, away from the demon, since it was provoking dissent. It's fighting Mal with the sword, trying to reach Candice. I don't think Mal is doing too well. It looks like they've stopped."

Sairis got to his feet. Marsden was already moving through the press of men and horses. Sairis followed, Roland on his heels. Everyone was, indeed, well back from the fight. Sairis couldn't see details, but Mal was on the ground. As he watched, the red knight drove the sword into the leopard's chest and jerked it free with a fierce cry. "There," he snarled, "now *you* can spend a thousand years inside a spirit vessel, you weak, human-loving alley cat."

The knight turned his attention to Candice, who was backing away. "Next," he hissed, "the little girl who should have stuck to embroidery."

The sword blazed all at once. The demon-knight jerked, but before he could drop it, necromantic fire raced up his arm. He howled, sounding entirely like the wolf. His shape disintegrated—a leaping, twisting form that rolled in the shallow water, but this was Karkaroth's own fire, his last outpouring of magic, and nothing could put it out. Demon and sword disintegrated in seconds, leaving behind nothing except a shapeless chunk of obsidian.

Sairis reached Mal, who appeared to be alive, though perhaps not for much longer.

Hastafel staggered away from Candice's advance, shock etched in his face. "You are a child!" he spat. "A...a little girl!"

"Perhaps," she said. "Perhaps that's why you chose me."

"What?"

"Gods," whispered Roland behind Sairis. He was looking at the remains of the sword, at the reflection spreading out from it along the surface of the water. Sunset colors disappeared, along with the reflection of the distant fort, and finally even the people standing in the shallow lake. Sairis saw a gray sky, twisted trees, and directly "above" them in the reflection, a tower collapsing, great chunks of masonry splashing soundlessly into a moat that was draining away.

A figure walked out of the tower—a familiar man, barely different from the one they'd been talking to a moment ago. Sairis remembered him pacing back and forth in his stone prison. *"Did I make more of them?"*

The man reached Hastafel in the reflection and vanished.

Lord Hastafel gave a jerk. His dark eyes went wide. He looked at the mirrored surface of the water. "No," he whispered.

He looked like he would run, but Candice snarled, "Stay, Phillip!"

"No, no, you can't... You have no idea! What do you want? Falcosta? I will make it yours. Your brother will fall at your feet or lose his head. Only let me close this weak place, this...this gate we have made by accident. It's...it's—"

"I don't want Falcosta," snapped Candice.

Another form materialized out of the tower beneath their feet—a younger warrior. *"Is there such a thing as enough power?"*

He disappeared, and Hastafel jerked again. He raised panicked eyes to Candice. "Do you want love? I know the name of another aspect of Lust—more sophisticated than that clown of a leopard. You will be desired by anyone you please. You will be coveted—"

"I don't want love," said Candice.

Another ghost appeared, this one a young scholar. *"This knowledge can't die with me."*

The sorcerer buried his face in his hands. "No, no, no…"

Another ghost, this one with a tear-streaked face, and then an animated one, looking around with anticipation. *"How many chances do you get at love?"*

Hastafel was sobbing. He curled over in the mud.

A sad-eyed ghost flitted past, looking like a lost child. And then, finally, the young shepherd. He stopped a pace from Hastafel in the reflection and looked at Candice for a long moment. "I have fulfilled our bargain," she said solemnly and Sairis's suspicion grew to a certainty.

"He gave you his name."

Candice nodded.

"He summoned Mal," said Marsden.

Another nod, and the goatherd smiled. "It's amazing what a man lets slip when he's only talking to himself."

Hastafel raised tortured eyes to his younger self. "Why are you doing this? We…we could have ruled the world."

"You imprisoned me!" hissed the boy. "You became just like those soldiers who burned our village."

"I did what had to be done!"

"I was a shepherd! You've become a wolf!"

"We will go mad!" cried Hastafel.

"Perhaps. It can't be worse than living the darkest day of my life forever."

He took the final step and vanished. Lord Hastafel froze, mute, his eyes wide, speechless with the memory of every part of himself he'd tried to forget.

A rasping voice. "Candice…?"

She whirled. "Mal."

Red mud slid under the leopard as he tried and failed to stand. Whatever else demons might be, they could apparently bleed. His pain appeared genuine as well. "You promised," he whispered.

Candice swallowed. "Could you heal yourself if you shifted?"

Mal smiled. "You promised," he repeated. "But sorcerers always lie."

Candice sniffled. "No, I…I'll do it. I'll miss you, that's all."

Mal's smile had a trace of something like sorrow. "I would have only devoured you in time."

"I don't believe that."

"Oh, believe it. Look at you. You don't even want sex, but you're half in love with me. I'd have you eating out of my hand before you knew it. I'd make you trust me. And then I'd eat you up. If there's one thing better than going home, it's going home with my master's soul in my belly." He ran his bloody tongue over his teeth.

In spite of this alarming speech, Candice knelt down beside his head. "You say the most awful things," she whispered. "But you've saved my life and kept me going when I would have given up. I will send you home, Mal, because I promised, but I don't think you're as heartless as you believe. I hope *you* fall in love someday." A hint of bitterness crept into her voice and she added fiercely. "I hope you fall so hard it breaks you!" She drew a deep breath and added, "Phillip Gosling, dismiss him."

Hastafel choked out a spell.

The leopard was staring at Candice the whole time, his face unreadable. He looked almost as though he intended to say something else, but then he vanished.

An instant's pause. "Well that was impressive," said Marsden. "Candice, are you—?"

"I am going to learn how to be a sorcerer," she said. "I am going to learn from the best."

"I'm not sure—" began Marsden.

"His ghost is fractured," interjected Sairis. "A spirit splintered for decades like that? He's never going to be sane!"

"Well, he deserves to die," said Candice frankly. "He's done terrible things."

Hastafel looked completely lost now. He was staring at his own hands. He got to his feet and turned in a slow circle, looking at the carnage of a battlefield as though he'd never seen such a thing before. "Where are the goats?" he whispered.

"Look at me," said Candice, and he turned obediently.

Hastafel's face cleared and there was a flash of the warlord. "You...contacted me. I thought..."

"Yes, you told me exactly what to write," said Candice. "Your younger self told me. He contacted me in the mirrors.

You were good at magic, even back then. It's a bad idea to be your own worst enemy, Phillip."

Hastafel opened his mouth as though to say something angry, then clasped both hands to his head and moaned. He doubled over again.

"You *do* deserve to die," continued Candice, "but you are going to live. Because *I* deserve a teacher. Inside that broken head of yours is everything I need to know about being a sorcerer. There aren't many of us in the world, and you're the best. So that is what you are going to do. After I put a proper collar on you."

"I am the one who will decide that." Daphne had ridden up. Sairis couldn't tell how much she'd heard, but clearly enough. "That man has caused immeasurable trouble, and you're not taking him anywhere, Candice."

Candice gave Daphne a sly smile. "Queen Daphne. I hope we can have pleasant dealings in the future. However, I am sorry to tell you that, yes, I am taking this sorcerer and leaving. I'll see that he never bothers you again." She stepped back, took Phillip by the arm, and vanished.

Daphne groaned. "Marsden, tell me they're just invisible."

Marsden cleared his throat. "I'm afraid not, Your Grace. She had a one-way jump spell. I learned about it when we helped each other during the fire. It's a single use gate. She could have gone anywhere."

Daphne made an exasperated sound. Behind her, sheepish-looking soldiers were forming up, trying to pretend they'd been ready to take on demons and wizards all along.

Daphne glared at Marsden a moment longer, but he looked back without a flicker. "Were you to hazard a guess at where she's gone," said Daphne with sarcasm, "where would that be?"

Marsden pursed his lips. "My guess would be very far from Mistala, Your Grace."

Daphne nodded. After a moment, she said, "Well, I believe we may say we have won the war."

"I believe that is true, Your Grace."

Sairis looked down and saw that the tower was in ruins, its reflection fading fast. As he watched, it melted away into ordinary sky, and the last of the sunset colors glowed in the remains of his wave. He let out a long breath, tension draining from his body. He still felt heavy, though. He suspected he would feel that way for a while.

Roland slipped an arm around his shoulders, and Sairis reached up to cover Roland's callused hand. He thought he should say something like, "I love you. I'm so glad you're alive," but instead, he said, "May I borrow Cato for a while?"

"Certainly. What are you borrowing him for?"

"I need to go home. I need to bury my master."

"Oh." A moment's surprised silence. "Do you know for sure that he's—?"

"Yes. Marsden can tell you about it. Right now, I just…I need to go home, Roland."

Roland walked him over to the horse. "I'll come with you. Let me get you supplies, food…"

"I'll stop by the wagons," said Sairis. *I'll live on magic if I have to. I've got plenty right now.* He pressed his fingers hard into the bridge of his nose to stop the stinging. *My teacher went down the River so that I didn't have to.* Aloud, he said, "I don't want company right now, Roland."

He finally risked a look at Roland's face and felt sorry for the hurt and concern he saw there. Sairis leaned up and kissed him on the cheek. "I'll come back."

"When?"

Sairis thought about it. "Two weeks. I'll meet you in Chireese." Then he climbed onto Cato, turned his back on the Malconwys, and headed home.

Epilogue

Roland Malconwy adjusted his linen cravat and flipped open one more button on his shirt as he strode into the Tipsy Knave. He hadn't bothered to wear the plainest clothes he could find. His waistcoat had a tasteful flourish of gold brocade over Mistalan green. His trousers were fitted to flatter a physique he'd earned in battle. His boots were tooled leather, and if one looked very closely, one might see the royal crest on his cufflinks.

Roland wasn't trying to hide, but he wasn't trying to flash his status, either. He hadn't worn a wig or a dress sword. At a distance, he might have been any well-turned gentleman out for the evening.

Nevertheless, a hush followed his passage through the tavern. Men pulled at their caps nervously, smiled, looked away. Roland inclined his head in return and ignored the more excessive gestures. When it was clear that he had no intention of holding court, the hush dissipated. The games of cards and darts resumed. In the corner by the fire, students shouted over one another in their discussion of the rumors that Lord Hastafel had returned to rule Zolsestron with a young female apprentice. Some said he was in love with her, others that she had him under a spell. It was all very juicy, and the students couldn't get enough.

Roland smiled. *Just a normal evening in the Tipsy Knave.*

Normal, except… It had been exactly two weeks from the day he'd watched Sairis ride off a drowned battlefield. Two weeks since he'd felt that kiss on his cheek. Two weeks since the last time Sairis had died and then come back before his eyes. *He does that far too often.*

"I have to go home, Roland." He'd been trying to go home since he arrived.

What if he doesn't want to come back?

Nevertheless, as Roland approached the bar at seven o'clock, he half expected to see a slim, dark figure in the corner already waiting for him.

The stool was empty.

Roland swallowed his disappointment and sat down. *It doesn't mean he isn't coming. He never told me when or where to meet. It's only sentiment that brought me here.*

Roland ordered a drink. He remembered his shock at finding Sairis on this same stool after he'd been stabbed. *He could barely stand, but he kept our date.*

Because he had nowhere else to go, whispered a voice in Roland's head. *You've been the only safe option for him at every turn. Do you really think he'd choose a knight and a Malconwy now that he has choices? He hasn't sent a single letter...*

Roland shut his eyes. *It's not easy to send letters from Karkaroth's wood. He's probably been busy.*

Nevertheless, persisted the voice, *what if he doesn't want you anymore?*

I wouldn't take anything back, thought Roland. *But I do hope we're still friends. I hope—*

Something moved in the spotty mirror behind the bar. Roland blinked. For one second, he could have sworn he saw the gray silhouette of a mouse, watching him. He turned and looked around the room again, but no one approached. He turned back to his drink and someone leaned across the counter. "Roland."

Roland looked up into dark eyes, luminous behind silver-rimmed spectacles. Roland wanted to stand up and pull him across the bar. "You came!"

Sairis broke into a grin that created points of light in his dark eyes. "I told you I would." He came around the counter. "I actually stayed here last night. I told the mouse to watch for you. The poor thing needs something to do. I waited far too long to banish it, and now it just seems determined to haunt the tavern."

Roland stood up and hugged him as he reached his stool. "I missed you," he said against Sairis's hair.

Sairis's arms folded tightly around his chest. "You haven't forgotten I'm a necromancer, right?"

"I have not forgotten. Does my horse still have fangs?"

Sairis smothered a laugh as he pulled away. "No. Although I may have fed him too many beans. Living horses are so inconvenient, what with all the feeding."

"Well, they smell better than dead ones, at least."

"Not when they've been eating beans. How is Butterball?"

"He is hale and hearty. Although I would like to give you a real horse."

"Butterball is a real horse!"

Roland smiled. Everything in the world seemed exactly as it should be. He was surprised to catch another familiar face at the end of the bar. "Is Marsden here?"

Sairis nodded. "I sent him a note when I got into town. He came over this afternoon to talk about the university. He wants me to help with some of the collared students."

"What did you tell him?"

Sairis shrugged. "I told him I'd try. He's right that some of them are dangerous, but keeping them collared will only make them resentful...or dead."

Roland nodded. "Daphne was asking whether it would be possible to place a magical perimeter around the whole kingdom."

Sairis frowned. "Ward the border? Yes, I suppose it's possible. It'd be a lot of work. And we'd have to renew them periodically."

"We could ride up along the Ridge Road this spring," said Roland with a smile. "Try it."

Sairis smirked. "I hear there are flowers."

"A few."

"And hot springs."

"We might have to stop at Mosshaven. Just because the trail is so dusty."

"Of course."

Marsden was talking to November and Hazel. A short, plump woman stood beside him. She had dimples and an impish grin. "Is that his wife?" asked Roland.

Sairis nodded. "I think November might like to try some glamours."

Roland chuckled. "I see where she and Marsden might have something to talk about." He was shocked when a young woman at the card table glanced his way and winked. The wink and tilt of the head were familiar, but the disguise was quite good. "Daphne?"

"Shhh!" hissed Sairis.

The gentleman across from her waved. He'd also gotten better at disguises. They no longer looked quite so much like frogs in fruit salad. Roland caught sight of Uncle Mani beside them, his head bowed over a pad of paper.

"I gather your only surviving uncle is still pining over a beautiful woman he met among the Falcostan emissaries," said Sairis.

Roland snorted a laugh. "Yes. Apparently Mal is a pretty unforgettable lay, although Uncle Mani is foggy on the details.

Marsden says that being fed upon by an astral demon can do that to you. He says Uncle Mani wasn't to blame, and he won't have any lasting ill effects. Which is good. Daphne and I have lost enough uncles lately."

Sairis scratched his head. "Did he draw pornography during meetings even before he bedded an astral demon?"

Roland passed a hand over his face. "Nearly always. Sairis, did everyone know you were coming here today except me?"

Sairis grinned, and Roland couldn't have held anything against him. "I wanted to surprise you," said Sairis. "I thought you'd like it if we all played cards."

"What if I hadn't come tonight?"

Sairis only smiled.

"Am I that predictable?"

"You're perfect."

Roland swallowed. "Sairis, something happened after you left. I saw...I saw Marcus in the water. Everyone was leaving, and nobody else saw him, but...I did."

Sairis's eyes studied Roland's face. He said nothing.

"I told him I love him," continued Roland. "And he sort of smiled at me. He said something, but I couldn't hear him. I think it was, 'I know.'"

"Of course he did," said Sairis softly. "You're not exactly subtle, Roland."

Roland forced his voice steady. "Then he disappeared. Do you think he's...alright?"

"His ghost is free. He was haunting Mount Cairn with a lot of other ghosts, and he helped me find the way down. He wanted vengeance for his murder and he got it."

"Marcus always was a stubborn bastard," observed Roland.

"I'm surprised he lingered so long afterward," continued Sairis. "He must have wanted very badly to tell you goodbye."

Roland wiped at his eyes. "But he's at peace now? The others, too?"

"Yes."

"The golems?"

"Gone. Exorcised. Down the River."

Roland nodded. That would have sounded like a terrible fate to him a month ago, but now... *I've seen the River. It's a good place to be...in the end.*

Sairis was speaking again. "I'm a little afraid that I might have created a weak place with my wave."

"A weak place?" echoed Roland.

"A spot where faeries or other monsters could cross over," said Sairis, "a thin spot between the worlds. I should take a look at it when we go on this warding tour in the spring."

Roland smiled.

Marsden, his wife, November, and Hazel had all joined Daphne, Anton, and Uncle Mani at the card table. They kept shooting glances at Roland and Sairis.

"I think we're wanted," said Sairis. "Unless you'd like to read my palm first."

Roland reached for Sairis's hand and folded it up between both of his.

"Looks difficult to read that way," said Sairis skeptically.

"It says you're coming home with me tonight," said Roland.

Sairis raised one eyebrow. "Spoken like a true knight."

"I can take no for an answer. Are you saying no?"

Sairis gazed up at him. Roland brought one hand gently to his jaw, and Sairis did not flinch. He did blink. His dark lashes brushed the silver frames of his spectacles. Roland leaned closer. "I want to kiss you. May I?"

"Yes," whispered Sairis.

His mouth opened like an invitation. Roland pulled him close, almost off the stool, and folded him up in his arms. He broke the kiss and whispered in Sairis's ear. "I want to play cards with our friends and drink and make jokes, possibly dance. And then I want to take you back to my bed—my *real* bed in the palace, not some hiding place. I want to kiss you everywhere and fuck you into the mattress. But if you don't want to, I am still happy beyond measure to see you tonight."

Sairis swallowed. "You can take me anywhere you like. Tied across your saddle, Roland."

"You don't sound sad about it."

"Not remotely."

Roland pulled away with a grin. "Then let's go see our friends."

Thank you for Reading The Knight and the Necromancer!

Would you like to spend a little more time with Roland and Sairis? Sign-up for the A. H. Lee newsletter https://www.abigailhilton.com/k-n

You'll get an exclusive second epilogue called "Spring in the Haunted Forest." You'll also get the prequel story "Putting the Romance in Necromancy."

Curious about What Happened to Mal?

You remember Candice's curse to Mal? "I hope you fall in love so hard it breaks you."

Well...

Mal has his own series. The story begins hundreds of years after Sairis and Roland's time. The series currently has 4 books plus a novella. It is MMF (two guys and a gal), and the MM portion doesn't really heat up until Book 2, but I promise you, it is worth the wait. Lots of feels.

The Incubus Series is a bit steamier than The Knight and the Necromancer (hey, it is about an Incubus), and it does include some sexy times with ladies. Book 1 - Incubus Caged - opens with one of the edgiest scenes I've ever written.

If you like my brand of storytelling, check it out.

Yours,

A. H. Lee

March 20, 2020

Manufactured by Amazon.ca
Bolton, ON